You Shouldn't Worry About the Frogs

YOU SHOULDN'T
WORRY ABOUT THE FROGS

Eliza Marley

QUERENCIA

Querencia Press, LLC
Chicago, Illinois

QUERENCIA PRESS

© Copyright 2023
Eliza Marley

ISBN 978 1 959118 25 1

www.querenciapress.com

First Published in 2023

Querencia Press, LLC
Chicago IL

Printed & Bound in the United States of America

For my family and friends who have endured many ramblings of fragmented stories in progress. Thank you for your unwavering support and love. Please know it is returned tenfold.

Contents

At the Bottom of the Cup

Anne always drove too fast. It was after midnight now and the road home was hazy with fog as it wound through the woods. There were no streetlights in the older parts of town, just cracked, glowing paint and the occasional rusted railing to remind you where the cliffs were. She had stayed too late at the shop again, reluctant to return to her dark and empty apartment. Anne yawned, keeping her eyes dead ahead where her high beams bounced off the fog and back towards her. A burst of dark brown fur rushed into view and Anne slammed on the breaks.

The deer stared at Anne, nostrils flared and eyes shining in the darkness. It was too thin, its fur matted and missing in patches. This is what happens when people build all sorts of new, fancy condos way out into the woods. All the animals get scared off and come running. Anne didn't really see the point of it all; it wasn't like they would be winning any metropolitan awards anytime soon. The poor thing was starving. It was probably trying to get someone to put it out of its misery. The deer tilted its head, a curious expression on its face. Everyone said you were just supposed to hit them, rather than risk swerving off the road. Anne beeped her horn and the deer sprinted away, disappearing again into darkness.

...

Madame Irva's Tea Room specializes in Psychic Tea Leaf Readings. It had all the essentials: dark curtains, burning incense, and a large crystal ball on the reading table that no one ever touched except when dusting. This was only Anne's second week working alone. Irva had left for a vacation to Florida with her husband. She had loaned Anne some dark lipstick and a couple of her blouses with long, flowy sleeves.

Anne was learning more about the art of tea leaves every day. It was interesting, and she was starting to understand why people got so into it. The problem was there were so many symbols and they always looked way clearer in the manual than they ever did in a teacup.

Now, there was a young woman across from her. She was chewing on her lip, tapping her fingers against the table. She had asked about where the tea they used was sourced from and if it contained sulfates. Anne was also chewing her lip, trying to maintain a sense of mystique as she tried to determine what the hell she was looking at.

Was it an apple? Or a circle? Maybe a lumpy smiley-face? What did those ones mean? The woman was watching intently and Anne was drawing a total blank. She plastered a smile to her face, hopefully looking like she was communing with the spirits themselves, and gently rocked the cup. Then, she carefully tilted it until some of the leaves spread out, thinner and thinner, keeping her sleeve out to cover the movement. Finally, one she knew.

"Alright my dear, you see the arrow here at the top of your cup?" Anne turned the cup around so the woman could see. The woman's brow creased and then smoothed again.

"Yes, I think so. What does that mean?"

"An arrow at the top of the cup usually means good news is coming your way."

"Does this mean I'll get the promotion?"

"Well, it can. But an arrow can also be a cautionary symbol, you may need to tread carefully with revealing your goals. It can also mean that you will be succeeding ahead of others. It's not pointed down, which is good. I'd say aim high, but don't put all your eggs in one basket."

The woman drummed her nails faster on the table, "So do you think I should ask to meet with my boss and ask him directly?"

"I would say let your work speak for itself for now, but don't be afraid to take an opportunity that presents itself to you." The woman must have decided that was an acceptable answer because she tipped with a ten before leaving.

Anne blew out the candles and switched on a small lamp. It was getting late and she doubted there would be any more walk-ins. Just as she got comfortable in her chair, the bell jingled at the front. She watched through the reflection on the crystal ball as a man walked in, tall and thin with his face hidden by hunched over shoulders and a mop of dark hair.

This was the most important part of any reading. Anne watched his distorted figure through the crystal ball as he stood stock-still in the shop, taking in his appearance. What would this man ask about? Money? Family? The man did not move, almost like he was hoping to just melt into the floor. No tells so far, he didn't even call out to see if anyone was in.

"One moment dear, I'll be right with you," Anne shouted. The man startled but did not look up. Well, he would be a surprise. Anne put aside her book and went to the front, pulling back the beaded curtain. "Welcome Sir, are you here for a reading?" The man nodded, never lifting his eyes from the floor.

"Wonderful, you can follow me back here and make yourself comfortable." Anne waved at the man to follow her. She left the lamp on. He didn't seem the type to care too much about ambiance.

They walked back to the reading table, the man dragging his feet across the carpet. He was dressed in a large brown sweater and loose, ill-fitting jeans, frayed at the bottoms.

The man sat down, finally lifting his head. He had deep circles under his eyes and a tiredness plastered to his face, giving his skin a sallow color. His chin and neck were stubbly and his lips were chapped. Anne cleared her throat, a little embarrassed. She was nothing much to look at either, so she really shouldn't judge.

"Have you ever had a tea leaf reading done before?" The man shook his head, still keeping his eyes down. "Well, I'm going to brew some tea and give you a small cup. I'd like you to drink most of it and think about what you would like to ask. Leave a little liquid at the bottom of the cup but not much, okay?" The man nodded.

Anne turned on the electric kettle and placed a pinch of dried leaves into a small teacup. "A lot of people ask about the future, if you're having trouble thinking of something. It doesn't have to be too specific so don't worry." The man nodded again, hands folded stiffly on the table. Anne poured the water over the leaves and handed it to him, still steaming. He drank in a slow, long sip and handed the cup back.

Anne knew this one. A skull at the bottom of the cup, small, scattered leaves around the rim. Danger coming from all sides. Beware. Emptiness. Doom.

Anne risked a quick look back to the man across from her. He had his eyes glued to his long, bony hands folded on the table. Anne shook the cup. She shook it until the leaves pulled in from the sides meeting at a lump in the middle. She tilted part of the lump until it fell away, creating a cleft in the middle. Anne cleared her throat, but the man still did not look up. "You're going to fall in love soon," she declared. The man's head whipped up.

"What?" his voice croaked out. He cleared his throat and coughed a couple times into his sleeve. "What did you say?"

"Do you see the heart in the middle of your cup?" Anne tilted the teacup towards him. The man shook his head.

"It just looks like mush to me, sorry."

"It's okay, here I'll show you." She traced the outline of a heart around the clump of leaves. "This means romance will be coming into your life, and from the placement in the cup, I would say it's coming soon."

"I'm going to fall in love?"

"You'll have the opportunity to fall in love, yes. These readings are not promises, but they can show you what's coming so you can look out for it. You don't want to miss any opportunities, right?" Anne offered him a small smile.

The man sat silent for a minute, brow furrowed. Anne wasn't sure what he had asked in the first place but hoped that her own divine intervention had at least made sense. The man suddenly hit his hands on the table, making Anne jump as he hastily stood up.

"Oh, I need to pay you for the reading. Sorry, it's so late, I'm sure you need to close or something." He walked briskly back to the front of the shop.

"It's okay, I always stay open late," Anne followed after him. "I'll make you a deal, okay? Come and see me again for another reading sometime and you can pay for that one. This one will be on the house," she said.

The man extended his hand. He smiled too, a small, awkward thing, but at least he was making eye contact.

"Cody. Thank you."

"Cody, a pleasure, my dear. Have a good rest of your night and remember to be open to opportunity."

Cody nodded and walked out into the night with his hands stuffed in his pockets. Anne watched him disappear from view and locked the door for the night.

...

Melanie was a regular on Wednesdays. Bubbly and gaudy, she was completely knowledgeable on all the symbols and meanings that Anne was only learning. She made Anne want to tear her hair out. Melanie had been coming in for a long time; apparently, she had once been engaged, but not anymore. Now she spent her time trying to dissect even the most arbitrary details of everyday life. Melanie sat at the table with her long, red nails wrapped around the sides of a full teacup as she continued to talk about, whatever she was talking about.

"You know, my dream last night was very insightful. I was surrounded by the color red and the sounds of a bird calling out to me in the distance. I cannot figure out what sort of bird it was though. I painted my nails red this morning just in case I'm supposed to be keeping the color near me." She wiggled her fingers.

Anne just nodded along, at least Melanie tended to talk her way through her own sessions without Anne having to gamble on saying the wrong thing. She took a sip of cooled tea, leaving a red lipstick print on the side of the cup. "I think it might have been a dove. You know, divinity and hope? Something good and powerful is coming my way, I'm sure. New love? Maybe I should dye my hair red? Or go to church? Oh, but the bird could have been a swallow or a parakeet. They all sound the same. Maybe I should get one for a pet? One of the little, yellow ones." Anne looked at the shiny, bird shaped brooch on her blouse. It looked like it was taking flight. "If it is a dove, then maybe I need to work harder at being, you know, pious or whatever. But, if it was a swallow, maybe now is a good time to travel and I should ask for vacation time. Maybe I should go to the park and feed the birds there."

"Maybe it was a gull," Anne offered.

"What do you mean?"

"Well, maybe the call you heard was a gull taking flight, freedom. Maybe you should be stepping back from looking for signs and remain open to adventure. Becoming too set on a single plan often leads to trouble." Melanie picked at her nails, taking another sip of her tea. "It sounds to me like you owe it to yourself to be on the best path, sometimes that means letting things come to you as they will, instead of seeking them out so aggressively."

"It could have been a gull," Melanie murmured. She set the cup down. "Actually, yes. I'm sure it was."

"Well then, just relax a little more and remain open to possibilities, my dear."

Melanie talked about gulls and where she could go for a spontaneous weekend trip, all the way back to the front. She turned to leave and walked right into Cody who was shuffling his way inside.

"I'm so sorry," Melanie said.

"Sorry, my fault," Cody stammered out. Melanie patted his shoulder.

"No, it was me, really."

"Cody, good to see you again," Anne said. He smiled.

"Thank you again," Melanie said. She moved past Cody and left. Cody stared after her and Anne cleared her throat behind him.

"I wasn't expecting you back so soon."

"Sorry, I couldn't remember the name of the place to look you up and see if I needed an appointment. I can come back another time."

"I'm free Cody, did you want another reading?"

"Yes please, thank you." Anne led him back to sit at the reading table. He was still wearing frayed jeans and his brown, stained sweater looked even worse in the daylight, but his hair looked cleaner and his eyes a little less sunken.

"You look well," Anne said.

"I've been getting more sleep."

"Good to hear," Anne handed him the teacup. "Now remember, think about what you want to ask. Drink the tea and leave a little bit at the bottom, okay?" Cody nodded and took the cup. He drank quickly and handed it back.

Anne was on a roll today. She hadn't even lied to Melanie, who knew what bird was in her dream? Besides, Melanie was smart and pretty, whatever she wanted she would probably get sooner or later. Cody was another story. He needed a push in the right direction. Anne peered into the cup and her smile dropped.

Small leaves scattered around the rim and a skull at the bottom. Danger coming from all sides. Beware. Emptiness. Doom.

"Do you still see love?" he asked softly. His eyes flickered up from the table to her, a curious expression on his face. Anne set the cup down.

"I see the possibility," Anne replied. "You need to work on being open, place yourself in the paths of others, and commit to being receptive to meeting new people. You will find the love I saw last time as long as you don't fall back on old habits. The leaves can't give you anything. At the end of the day, you have to go and get it for yourself, Cody." He exhaled in a long, slow breath.

"Thank you," Cody replied, eyes on the table. He didn't ask any other questions.

"I hope you come back again," Anne said after Cody had paid at the front.

"I'll try my best."

After Cody left, Anne made some more tea. She let hers steep much longer than she did with clients, waiting until it was nearly opaque. Anne gulped down the tea until she tasted the bitterness of the leaves. She pushed her cup to the side without looking at what was left. Cody's cup was still sitting on the table. The leaves had dried, sticking to the bottom in their skull shape. Anne grabbed her coat and went out for a walk.

The park down the road had a crowd gathered around it when Anne walked past. There were the flashing lights of an ambulance along with a couple officers spreading yellow tape in front of the onlookers, pushing them further back. Anne crossed over and tried to see what was going on. An older woman turned to her, "There was an accident," she said.

"What happened?"

"There was a young lady standing on the bridge. A goose flew right at her and she fell back into the water. A man jumped in after her. Someone got the girl out, but the man died, I think. I'll bet he hit his head on the rocks. The water in that pond is pretty shallow."

Anne looked past the woman with a funny feeling in her stomach. The bridge was arched over a lily pad pond and painted bright red. There were EMTs standing over someone laid out on a tarp. Anne walked closer and saw one of them zipping a body bag over a wet, brown sweater.

She ended up leaving the shop closed the rest of the day. She drove home slowly, looking out at the half-constructed apartment complexes and the long stretches of dense forest in between. The sun was shining through small gaps in the trees. As she passed around a bend, she saw the dead body of a deer slumped off to the side. Anne sped up.

Chewing On It

Emma made a face at the little, green leaf floating in her latte foam. The sweet smell wafting up from the cup made her stomach churn. She had made the drink herself with extra foam and a healthy sprinkle of cocoa powder on top, just the way she liked it. Emma tossed the garnish on without a thought, a tragic byproduct of muscle memory that had now ruined her perfectly good latte. She took her spoon and pushed the offending leaf all the way down to the bottom of her cup before standing and throwing the whole thing away along with a barely picked-at scone.

Sprigs of the plant were sitting in fancy, glass vases on every table. Their leaves wiggled slightly under the breeze created from the ceiling fan. Just when she thought they couldn't find any more ridiculous ways to force it on everyone, they kept surprising her. Emma was having none of it.

"You sure take short lunch breaks," Jamie said. She was leaning back against the counter, waiting for a panini to finish in the press. Emma adjusted her apron as she returned to her station near the bakery case. "Did you even eat anything?"

24

"I'm not too hungry," Emma replied, "Besides, I like making the coffees more than I like drinking them."

"Well, lucky for me, I hate that milk steamer. It burned me again last week!" The chimes on the front door jingled, "Look, here comes Mr. Charles, right on time." Jamie went to take the man's order. He owned the local market and was nice enough but kept his eyes a little too low for Emma's taste. He ordered the fish and chips as always with a large iced-mocha and a wink to Jamie that she politely smiled at. Mr. Charles went to find a table and Jamie turned back to Emma to stick her tongue out in a fake gag. Emma made the drink quickly, plucking off a few green leaves from a bundle of the plant Brandy had left at the station and sprinkling them on top to finish it off.

"How long do you think Brandy is going to make us use this stuff?," Emma asked. "It's messing up my artistic vision. She even made me put it on top of the blueberry muffins. Who garnishes a muffin?"

"I don't know, it's fancy or whatever. Besides, it's just like using mint."

"It's not the same and you know it." Emma's eyes moved over and out the window to the park bench across the street. She could almost picture the hunched over figure sitting down, shaggy gray hair and an old army coat, spitting out chewed-up mint leaves all over the place. "He died there. It's creepy."

"Well, I think it's sort of cool," Jamie said. "Plus, business has picked up since we started using it. I'm not mad at these tips." The fish came up from the fryer, complete with chopped up, little green leaves on top. Looking at the things, slightly wet with fry grease, made Emma choke back a gag. She took a deep breath to calm her stomach and focused her gaze outside at the park.

There were people walking through, stopping to sit in the grass and enjoy the spring weather. It was more crowded now than it had ever been. Every now and then, someone would bend down beside a park bench and pluck some of the plant straight from the ground. There was a small crowd patiently chatting while they waited for a turn. Emma suddenly felt the urge to get away from the windows and mumbled something to Jamie about rolling out dough for cherry pies as she fled to the kitchen.

Davie had been a regular, sort of. He would linger outside by the front, staring at everyone who walked by, muttering to himself, before making his way over to his usual spot on that park bench across the street. He always sat at the same bench. He would stare into space and mutter more there, always chewing raw mint leaves the way other people chewed tobacco. Chew, spit, mutter, and shout. He shouted about a lot of things. Mostly God, sometimes the end of the world, or how men from the telephone company were coming to kill him. A lot of people avoided the park altogether. Emma was always the first to arrive at the diner to start baking for the day and she would give him a fresh danish and a to-go coffee. He never thanked her and usually sent her away with a brisk wave and a muttered curse.

Davie died on that bench. Emma tried to think of it like he died at home. The city had the whole thing cleaned professionally afterwards; the park district even paid to have flowers planted around the walkways and a new water fountain put in. A couple weeks later, the plant started sprouting up all around Davie's bench. It looked like mint from far away, but up close you could see the leaves were longer. They curled and twisted in strange ways, looking accusatory. It grew in patches, crawling all over the grass, but never more than a few yards away from Davie's bench.

It creeped Emma out, but everyone else in town loved it. They hung it in garlands, added it to floral bouquets, and served it in lemonades. It was getting to be a little much, honestly. She had even heard Brandy talking about adding it into pancake batter. Every morning, Emma came to work and hurried past the park. She pointedly ignored the curly, crinkled leaves and the now empty bench.

...

Mr. Brian Porter, The Junior Parks Supervisor, was thrilled. He'd been content when the hobo man had died, God rest his soul. A tragedy, of course, but it filled him with glee to think that maybe the park could be used for more productive matters without that vagrant yelling and scaring people off all day and night. It was the last thing a small town needed—aggressive drifters. He'd taken it upon himself to have the whole area sanitized. He'd made PowerPoints full of proposals from weekly summer concerts to crafts fairs. He'd even hired landscapers. It was the biggest park in town, three miles of sheer potential right in the center of most of their shops and restaurants. It was time for it to be treated with respect.

The problem was that people kept leaving. All the young people, the good people with skills and aspirations. They had no interest in giving back to their community. It could be fixed however, if they created the right environment to shmooze them into staying put. In a park you could have arts festivals, farmers markets, and even club sports. Structured activities were the sorts of things one looked at when deciding on committees and elected officials, after all. The weird plant had been a surprise bonus.

A couple weeks after cleaning up the park, a sort of weed sprouted up all around the vagrant's bench. At first, Mr. Porter had them ripped out, but they just crept back stronger by the next morning. They spread all the way around that damned bench, crawling along the ground like clover, but stopped a couple yards away, forming a near circle around it. It grew low to the ground in thin, curly leaves. If he looked from the right angle, the leaves looked a bit like fingers, reaching out towards the sky. Mr. Porter didn't like to look at it too long.

"It tastes just like mint," Jones, one of the gardeners, had told him.

"You mean you ate some of it?" he questioned, gobsmacked.

"Tastes fine, is all I'm saying. You might as well just leave it, it won't hurt nobody." Mr. Porter could not believe anyone would willingly eat an unknown plant. He had thought about it all day. He told his wife about it that night and she immediately wanted to try some herself. She picked a handful and passed it around to the ladies at her bridge game. It did, in fact, taste just like mint. She said it had been a real hoot—the ladies ended up fashioning a round of juleps with it.

Mr. Porter started to form an idea. This was just like that city up north, where the woman had died in her apartment and no one had found her for months. She rotted away to bones still wearing her church shoes, sitting in her favorite chair. When they had finally cleared the place out, people flocked to stay there for a night. Ghost enthusiasts and devil worshippers, not really the sorts of people he wanted in his town, but Mr. Porter believed he could work with it. This was natural after all. It was a locally sourced crop, brought into existence by the departed spirit of a beloved local. The whole thing was sort of divine, really.

Mr. Porter set up a meeting with Brandy, who'd been running Tad's place since his heart attack. He invited Williette from the dinner club, Ben from the radio station, and Father Beckitt of the local parish too. Mr. Porter cheerfully pulled out a bundle of the plant he had picked on the walk over and tossed them into everyone's salad bowl. Here, was the opportunity of a lifetime. A way to bring people together over a common product for the good of their town. What was better than that?

...

Emma swallowed down against her nausea, looking over the tray of muffins she had baked that morning. They looked beautiful, perfect, with crispy brown tops and just a hint of red berries leaking through the wrappers. But the sweet, minty smell of the plant leaves scattered on the tray stuck in her nose and overpowered everything else. People had taken to calling the stuff 'Davie's Hands'. Emma adamantly refused to go along with it. Maybe her anger was unjustified. She had never really spoken to the man and gave him the same wide berth everyone else did, but she had always felt they had an understanding with one another. Emma had the feeling that Davie had been someone before he ended up in town. She wondered where he had been, if it was anywhere Emma might see one day. Probably not.

Emma couldn't sit still for long without feeling like people were watching her. She could be completely alone and still feel eyes burning into her skin, wordless and faceless beings sneering from the shadows. She could never last long enough to eat a meal or finish a book. Anytime she wasn't busy doing something her skin started to buzz and her breath came short. Here, Emma could stay busy. If someone was looking, she would be doing something impressive. She could swirl frosting and crimp crusts all day long. And then, people could coo over the pretty buttercream roses and focus on the fresh muffins. They wouldn't pay attention to her at all.

"Do you want to go on break first today?" Jamie asked. She had come in late that morning, last night's makeup still smudged around her eyes and her hair in a haphazard bun.

"No, I'm not sure I'll take one today. I'm feeling a little restless, I might go back and make some whoopie pies. Holler if we get busy?"

"Alright, just let me know if you feel sick, and remember to eat something."

Emma kept busy all day, rolling out dough, cutting biscuits, and putting together fruit tarts. Each item was to be topped with a little bit of the plant. Emma set a whole leaf on top of a cupcake, noticing that it really did look like fingers up close. It sat curled on the frosting, wiggling gently from the kitchen fan, like it was beckoning her forward. She ended up chopping them up into thin strips for the rest.

Emma declined a ride home from Brandy. She stayed late, drinking a cup of tea and nibbling a piece of toast in the dark, empty kitchen. When she finally started the walk home, Emma took the long way, avoiding the park, and curving through the streets of town. She peered into dark windows at drawn curtains and hanging bushels of the plant left in doorways. Father Beckitt had started proclaiming hanging a bunch over your front door would bring good luck and now every building had one. The leaves were strung into garlands, weaved around streetlights, and draped over railings. The leaves waved in the wind and cast fluttering shadows onto the street which Emma stepped over.

She walked until she found herself at the church's gate across town. Davie's grave was in the back of the churchyard, a rough, brick-red stone paid for by the congregation. No one had known when he was born so it

32

just read -Davie- with a cross carved in at the top. She patted the bare headstone and noticed something sprouting up at the base. It was a small cluster of the plant. She had never seen it anywhere else except the park around Davie's bench. Emma plucked a leaf off and sniffed it. The plant smelled like regular mint. She popped it into her mouth, ready to see what the fuss was all about. It burned on her tongue and Emma spat it back out.

...

Mr. Porter had decided that he was a genius. The people loved "being in Davie's Hands", as Father Beckitt had called it earlier at mass. It was their own local miracle! A television station up North was even coming down next week to do a feature. Mr. Porter himself didn't care for it, the minty smell made his nose itch, but his people were consuming the stuff by the bushel. They picked their leaves fresh, stuck them in smoothies and breakfast burritos. They crushed it and used the oil in candles and soaps. They dried it and hung it in their windows for luck.

The park had families in it, everyone stopping in to pick their fill. If you stayed all day you could even watch the plant regrow itself, crawling along the earth as new leaves unfurled. Soon, after charging a small harvesting fee, they could buy one of those big screens and show outdoor movies. Mr. Porter was filled with ideas, a whole binder in fact, ready to be taken before the board at their next monthly overview meeting.

After a successful day out in town, Mr. Porter came home. He read a book, drank a warm glass of milk, and worked on a crossword puzzle. He laid beside his wife who had been asleep since he had gotten in. He dropped a kiss to her hair and drifted off himself.

Usually Stella woke up before him, but the next morning he could still feel the weight of her next to him in bed. He rolled over to wake her up, except when he reached out a hand, she was cold. Mr. Porter had to steel himself to take a closer look. She laid there, not breathing, no heartbeat, completely frozen. The shape of her was exactly right, with her closed eyes and wrinkled forehead, but her skin and hair was gray and rough to the touch. She had turned to stone. He shook her. He pulled at her arms. When she wouldn't budge, Mr. Porter got out of bed and put on his shoes. He left the house in his pajamas and started walking towards downtown.

Mr. Porter ran into Sammy Franklin next, also turned to stone. He was stuck looking out from his window, squinting and waving down at Miss Nadia from the bank. She had not seen him waving yet. She was frozen facing down, holding her skirt, picking her foot up to step over a dip in the sidewalk.

Next came Mrs. Adams, who was stock-still in the middle of her morning walk. In her hand she held a sprig of Davie's Hands, still fresh and green, waving in the breeze like Miss Nadia's skirt. Mr. Porter kept walking and he found Brandy. She had a hand stretched out towards the side door of Tad's, her key held in unmovable fingers. Paula from the butcher's sat in the park, a packet of bird seed dropped next to her along with three stone pigeons. As Mr. Porter made the rounds through town, it became clear that everyone was gone. Well, everyone was here. The faces of his people forever set in calm, blissful smiles. A sea of blank stares that peered out into nothingness from gray, unflinching eyes.

Mr. Porter wished to be stone as well. Back home again, he looked over his wife and thought maybe he could lay back next to her, close his eyes, and it would take him too. It didn't, so he packed a small bag and headed for the train station. He walked through the park, stopping to pick a candy bar wrapper out of a flower bed and throw it away. He passed the bench and saw that the plant had finally crawled far enough without interruption to wrap itself around the legs of the bench. Davie's Hands curled around the bench legs, green leaves gripping tightly enough to splinter the wood.

...

Emma left for work later than usual. The few hours of sleep she had gotten settled behind her eyes like a buzz. She walked towards town enjoying the slowly rising sun. Its hazy, pink light gave her an idea for an upside-down plum cake she would try to make later. Something with a honey glaze on top that would look just like the sunbeams casting rays on the sidewalk. Emma noticed Paula was already sitting at the park with her bird seed.

"Good morning," Emma offered. Paula didn't answer her. Emma stepped forward and her foot knocked against something hard. She looked down to see a large rock, no, a bird at her feet. It was a startlingly realistic pigeon.

"Wow, some carving, huh?" Again, there was no answer. Emma finally raised her head to meet Paula's eyes. They were flat and gray. Emma realized with a bolt of shock running through her that she could not remember what color they were supposed to be. Now, Paula was just hard concrete all over. She reached out to jostle Paula's statuesque shoulder, but it didn't give.

Emma backed away and then ran across the street to the diner. Brandy was out by the door, key stuck in her frozen hand. There was no sign of Jamie at all. Emma ran away from her, down the main street and passed by a few others who were also all stuck like statues. She tried shaking a couple, but no one even budged. Was she dreaming? Hallucinating? Was she turning into stone too? Emma ran a hand down her sweaty face. The sun had risen higher, casting shadows off of the stony faces of people she knew and onto the street. Emma felt her racing heart and the pull of her lungs in her chest. She didn't feel like stone. Slowly, she walked back to the diner.

She scooted around Brandy and went inside. The diner was dark and empty as it was each morning. Emma took her proofed bread dough out to rest on the counter. She prepped some vegetables and put a round of danishes in the oven to bake. In the dining area, she flipped on the lights and pulled back the curtains. Across the street, she could see the back of Paula's petrified head facing away.

Emma was about to turn away when she saw the man from city hall running through the park. He wasn't stone either, then. She thought about going after him, saying something, but she couldn't remember his name. She let him go and watched as he disappeared across the park. Emma stayed in the window, waiting to see if anyone else would pass by, but no one did. Eventually, the timer for her danishes went off. After taking them out, she rummaged around the fridge and pulled out some eggs, mushrooms, and cheese. Emma's stomach rumbled.

As her eggs cooked, Emma walked up to the front
and flipped the Closed sign to Open. She turned her
omelet out onto a plate, perfectly golden and steaming.
She left off the garnish and went to sit down at a booth
with her plate and a bowl of sliced watermelon. She faced
out towards the park and took a bite of eggs, promising
herself that the next person to come by, she'd get up and
say something. For now, it looked like she had time to sit
and eat for a while.

Mise en Abyme

I.

There is always a chance, statistically insignificant but not impossible, that when you go to kick a wall your foot may go completely through instead of bouncing off. I remember that line from a late night infomercial, maybe it was for one of those tupperware things. There is always the possibility that something may not be where it should be. I used to use that line when I misplaced my keys.

I had swung my legs out of bed like always, with my hip I have to do things slowly. When I didn't feel my foot, I'd figured it was just poor circulation. It's not uncommon for me to have to lie in bed for a little and let my fingers and toes stop tingling. But when I got up I almost fell back over and had to brace myself on the nightstand. When I looked down, I thought I'd have a heart attack.

My left foot was completely gone.

It didn't fall off or anything either, I checked. All that was left was the very end of my ankle, rounded off like someone had come along with an eraser.

No drugs either, not for me. I've got a severe allergy to whatever it is they put in those plastic capsules these days. And I sure didn't sell it to anyone either. I knew a girl, Martha, and she swore up and down that a man she had met online stole one of her kidneys. Of course, she was a bat and didn't even know where her kidneys were. But, then she had a stroke, so I'm not allowed to say anything about it.

That first morning, I looked down at my new ankle stump and felt exhilaration. I'm a little ashamed to say it, what with all those charities and stuff out there, but I felt great. I'd lived my whole life as ordinary Linda, married Linda, and widow Linda. Now, I was one-footed Linda, and that just seemed so much more interesting. I hadn't felt so good since I fit into a size eight jeans.

I didn't know where to go first. I wasn't seeing any of my friends until Wednesday when the home April and Charlie lived in hosted Canasta. I thought about calling my granddaughter, but she was always busy, and my son worked day and night. I had nowhere else to show it off, so I went to get some groceries. I put on one of my nice, strappy sandals even though it was too cold for them. I kept myself steady with Rick's cane; they gave it to him when he first got sick. It was a little too tall for me, but the wobbling added to the look.

It's not every day something life changing happens and I deserved to bask a little. But nobody even noticed.

I'll tell you, if Marnie was here, she would have gotten everybody's attention. She's stuffed up with fillers the way a jumbo shrimp is stuffed with cream cheese. If she walked in here, everybody would hold out a hand and offer to push her cart.

I've never been much of a head turner, but with Rick at least I always had somebody with me. It's been about three years but it's still hard sometimes. He always kept tissues in his sleeves and would tell me when I needed to touch up my lipstick. He smelled like licorice, even in his younger days. I loved that about him.

I was walking through the aisles, not really looking, when I saw another woman trying to grab a pack of frozen corn. Her black, billowy sleeves were too long and kept catching on the shelves. I hobbled over to her and tapped on the glass door she was holding open with her hip.

"Can I give you a hand?"

"Excuse me?" She snapped at me and then let the door slam shut. "Do you think that's a funny thing to say to me?"

"I'm sorry. I was just trying to help you."

"Well, I don't need any help!" She shooed me off with both arms and when her sleeves flew back, I could see the rounded end of a wrist with no left hand attached to it. She saw me staring and pulled her sleeve back over the stump, embarrassed.

"Can I ask you something?" I asked, excited.

"What?"

"I don't want to be rude but...did your...did it just go missing one day?"

She stared back at me. Her eyes traveled across my face and down my body. I waited as she finished her scan and took a step back. I thought she would yell again but she started to laugh, "Did you..."

"Just this morning," I replied. Her laughter was contagious.

"I've never seen anyone else—well, I've never asked before."

Her name was Mary, she was 48, and she had a face that looked like it hadn't seen a smile in years. She had puffy cheeks that stretched down to a tight-lipped mouth and a few hairs on her chin. We finished our shopping together, talking the whole time. The two of us, her with no hand and me with no foot, turned more heads than I ever imagined. People stared, gawked even, and I tried to stay sensitive enough to muster a blush about it.

It came easier to Mary; she kept her sleeve draped over the stump and would not meet anybody's questioning gaze.

We went out for coffee after the store, letting the bags of frozen produce melt in her trunk as we talked some more. We met up every day the rest of that week.

Mary mostly talked about her daughter. She had been missing for fifteen years since disappearing on the way to a friend's house. She had given Mary a ring for Mother's Day when she was little, and Mary never took it off. It was a plastic ring with big, fake gems on it that sparkled insistently no matter how dark the room was. She said it happened a few years ago, on the anniversary of her disappearance. Mary had just woken up and the hand was gone. The ring was sitting in the sheets of her bed, so she started wearing it on the other hand.

Mary lived in an apartment by herself, just like me, but hers was on the other side of town. It was small and poorly decorated, but it was the only place she could relax in. I was always talking about how she needed to get out more, but she could get so stubborn. So, we would sit in her living room on her lumpy couch and drink tea. I showed her a picture of my granddaughter and Mary talked about how she used to braid Hayley's hair for school.

After a month of trying, I finally brought her out for cards. All the girls were there and they just loved Mary. They called us the dynamic duo and Marnie even asked to feel Mary's stump. Alice made a joke about reading her palm and I could tell Mary just loved being around the group. People have to be around other people or they just wither away.

I don't think Mary saw it that way. After the card game she stopped returning my calls. I gave it a few weeks, calling and asking around about her at the store and the coffee shop, but no one had seen her. I was getting worried, so I dropped by her apartment. The door was unlocked the way she always left it. I looked around but there was no sign of Mary anywhere. She had left a cup of tea in the microwave and her electricity was shut off. I was about to leave, give up for good, when I saw a colorful reflection off the framed school picture she had of Hayley hanging on the wall. It was coming from her bed. I ruffled through the sheets until finally, Mary's ring came tumbling out, daintily placed on the single finger still attached to it.

I'm pretty sure that's all that's left of her. I think everything just got to be a bit too much for Mary. I don't know if she can hear me or feel me there, but I just can't bear to let her go. I keep her with me now, in a nice little tin in my purse. I make sure she stays clean, and I even paint her nail every now and then when I get lonely. It's nice to have someone with me again.

II.

It was the first time the traveling magician had planned ahead for a show. He would go from town to town alone, doing tricks in the parks and empty, rural lots for children passing by. The swatches of green and brown country roads were his home and he never stayed in the same place for more than a few nights. Families would always try to hire him to do birthdays, but he never accepted any jobs or money, not even a tip off the street. But this town loved him more than all the others and he wanted to show them something truly amazing. He had some of the children put up posters all over town about a magic show in the park that night. It was the most exciting thing to happen since a circus with real elephants had come through last summer.

He wore a black suit with a single red flower on the lapel. He was very quiet and polite, raising his hat to the ladies walking with their daughters to the corner store. Anyone who might have been suspicious about the tall stranger in a small town would be immediately won over by his quiet, constructed, closed-lip smile.

As the sun was setting, nearly the entire town came to a small park by the community center. Only a few families, with children sick from the flu going around town, stayed behind. The contagious children all wallowed in their disappointment, but there was one little girl, a bright and curious child, who was not to be deterred by imposed bedrest.

She had seen the man once during the last time he came through town. The man had walked down the road and stopped to talk to her. She remembered him complimenting the ribbon in her hair and making a quarter appear from thin air which he gave to her for candy at the store. She liked the man and wanted to see him again. So, with her runny nose and fever-red cheeks, she slipped out the back door after her mother had tucked her in.

The show was lit by torches stuck in a field used for soccer practices. The air was cool and the sound of crickets permeated the silence of a crowd waiting to be amazed. People were sitting on blankets and lawn chairs the same way they did for the Fourth of July, some even brought sparklers. The magician stood before them all. In the darkness, only the red flower of his jacket stood out, gleaming in the fire's light.

He began by making one of the torches fly. It soared through the crowd, minding the women's hair and the children's grabbing hands, and landed at the man's feet. He did card tricks, illusions, and cut the librarian, Renee, in half like she was butter. When she got out of the box she took a bow, and the magician pulled another flower from his sleeve for her. It was pink like her blush when she took it.

The girl arrived at the show about halfway through. She was entranced by the sparkling lights and the rabbit pulled out of the man's hat. He barely said a word, only bellowed with joy when the town applauded him.

Finally, it was time for the last trick. He asked for a volunteer and the girl shot her hand up, waving it wildly, but she was too far back for him to see. A chubby little boy made his way to the front to take the magician's outstretched glove instead.

The magician produced a mirror from his back pocket. It started out as a small square in the palm of his hand with a delicate, silver frame. And then he shook it. It became clearer, bigger, and by the time he was done it was a full-length mirror that the man held up and turned to face the boy. He asked in a low voice for the boy to stick his hand into the mirror. The boy did. The magician turned the mirror so the crowd could see that the boy's hand was not coming out the other side. It was somewhere else. The magician asked the boy to stick his other hand into the mirror. The boy did. Then the magician asked the boy to stick his entire head into the mirror. The boy did, and as he stood there, half way inside the mirror, most of the audience regained their belief in real magic.

After the show, the families packed up and left. Children swung on their parents' arms, excitedly recapping all the tricks they had just seen. But the girl stayed behind, walking against the flow until the field was empty and she stood before the magician. He looked down to her with a soft gleam in his eye and pulled another red flower out from his sleeve.

The girl took the flower but continued to stand there, looking over the tall man in the dark suit. The magician put a single, gloved finger to his lips and the girl repeated the gesture, giggling as she copied him. The magician pulled from his pocket the same mirror as before, shaking it out to full size, and facing the girl with it. In the mirror, she saw herself and the darkness of the barren field around her. She looked up at the man and he nodded. The girl tapped the surface of the mirror, and it rippled like water. She rubbed it and it felt like glass.

The girl slowly put one arm into the mirror. It felt warm and airy, like the front porch of her house where she would sit in a rocking chair with her mother. The girl put her other arm into the mirror and felt the soft leaves and small thorns of a blackberry bush, so much like the one that grew in her front yard. The girl took a breath and put her head into the mirror.

According to the town, she just got lost. The official story is she wanted to see a friend, but with her fever she must have forgotten the way. She probably wandered away into the woods and fell into the river or fell asleep under some bushes. The gossipy old ladies would say she was eaten by a mountain lion. No one thought anything more than that. Surely, there was no one here she would have gone off with, no one that would not have returned her had they found her.

No one could ask the magician because he never came back. He left town that same night, walking the familiar tree-lined roads to some other, sleepy town. Even if someone had asked, it wouldn't have led to anything. The man would've leaned down with his soft smile and gloved hands to give them a glimmer of something wonderful. And then, he would have brushed the dust off his suit jacket and carried on his way, somewhere else.

III.

Wendy was looking at me from across the table, eyes wide and glasses falling off her nose. It was only our third date. We usually went to the taco truck, but tonight I pushed for Italian. It was the new place in town, nicer. Plus, it guaranteed me more time with her if we had to sit down in the squeaky, too-big booth.

"Do you ever wonder if someone's hiding out there, just waiting to kill you?" She raised an eyebrow as she said this, trying to be dramatic.

"Like a horror movie or something? The psycho killer always knows where you are?" I met Wendy at comic book club. There are only a few sure-fire ways to meet cute, Queer girls on a college campus this far out in Iowa. She loved fantasy books and had an overactive imagination that almost made up for my own complete lack of creativity.

"I was walking home the other night by Mason Street, you know, with all the corn fields. I was walking alone and thinking, what if someone just popped out from the corn right now and grabbed me?"

"Well, if they're popped, all you need is the butter."

"Be serious Colleen, I mean like a man or something."

I took a sip from my soda. Wendy said the word 'man' in a whisper, like one might be lurking somewhere, listening. I looked around the sparsely populated restaurant to make sure the coast was clear before turning back and motioning her to continue.

She giggled, "I was thinking, maybe if someone did try to attack me, I could karate chop them or something. I'd be ready. I'd open my purse and pull out a machete. Then, I would swing it around, and he'd try to run at me, but I'd slice off his head. Or I'd chop off his arm and he'd run away screaming, leaving a trail of blood behind for the police to track."

"That sounds like a reasonable plan to me."

"But I don't have a machete. Even if I did, it wouldn't fit in my purse, and I wouldn't know how to use it."

I pushed the basket of breadsticks towards her. "Practice with these."

She laughed, her hair getting close to falling into her food. "If you're worried about something like that, start carrying around pepper spray. Or I'll just escort you everywhere, like a big, buff bodyguard."

Wendy nibbled on a breadstick, the end of one curl dipping slightly into the marinara sauce.

"Please, like you'd do any better than me in a fight." I sat up a little taller in my seat.

"I could fight a bear if I needed to," I wanted to add 'for you' but brushed the hair out of her food instead.

There was a moment of comfortable silence while we ate. It was so natural to sit here with her, but I couldn't help my eyes drifting up to the mirrored ceiling of the restaurant. There was another couple, a few booths away, well into their meal. I watched the woman with long, dark hair twirl her spaghetti upside down. When I looked back down Wendy was smiling at me, her food abandoned.

"You really don't get thoughts like that? Like any moment you could be out grocery shopping or walking to your car and someone just tries to grab you?"

"I don't know what they'd want with me. I have heard about that car stuff though. I hear they hide under your car and wait for you to walk up to it. Then, they cut you at the ankle so you can't run away. I guess there's some ligament there or something."

Wendy was staring at me and clutching her napkin in her hands. Backtrack.

"But hey, you don't even have a car here, so you don't have to worry about that."

Wendy just sighed. "I know it's stupid. It just makes my skin crawl. I remember last week I was grocery shopping in the middle of the day and this guy at the counter was so nice to me. He was asking me how I was, if I got everything, and gave me the deal on my coupon even though it had expired. But then, as I was leaving he asked for my number, and I did the whole, 'Sorry, I'm gay' thing, but then I swore I saw him again later at Walgreens and again when I was walking to ceramics class. And I started thinking, what if he's following me?"

"Maybe he just needed cough drops?"

"I know I'm being paranoid. It's a small campus anyways. It just made me stop for a second. What would I do if I was being stalked? Proper stalked. Where they send you pig hearts in the mail and letters written in their own blood and cut up magazines."

"I guess it could happen. Maybe every time you look out the window they're out there. But only for a second. Just long enough to make you feel crazy. And then they seduce a plastic surgeon to make a clone of you."

"I would freak if someone ever made a clone of me."

"I better not take you back to my dorm room then," I wiggled my eyebrows at her and felt a pang of success when she laughed.

"Tell me another one." Wendy was twirling pasta around on her fork, playing with it.

"Another creepy story?"

"Yeah, you're good at it."

"Alright." I pulled on my sleeve.

It started with footsteps. Boots on an empty sidewalk, late enough that the crowds of drunken kids outside the bars had gone home. Boots that were too big because men's sizes were wider, and women's had too many sparkly buckles. It was cold too. Boots on a sidewalk, echoing in the familiar pattern of hurrying home and out of the wind. An arm stretched across a flannel, clutching it to a chest to keep warm.

And then more steps, different steps.

A different type of cold and the familiar urge to turn around and glare. Of course it was a man, dark jacket, face obscured in the shadows. You could never see his eyes. The arm holding the flannel clutches tighter and the footsteps speed up.

The man laughs or maybe he doesn't. He speeds up or maybe he doesn't. Everything that happens next is filtered through the rough breaths, exhaled in soft puffs into the empty air. Eyes searching for others, seeing nothing but dark store fronts and neon signs.

There are conflicting rhythms, the two sets of steps, unevenly matched, and the sudden racing of a heart. Why didn't I wear a bra? Suddenly, there weren't enough layers. My hips flattened in loose jeans, but there. My hair, stuffed into a baseball hat but coming loose and hanging down my neck. Suddenly a woman, walking home alone and a man walking behind her, in the dark.

"Colleen, I was just kidding. You don't actually have to think up another murder story."

The soft background music and the sound of people talking around us rushed back in. I realized I had been staring into space. I looked back up to the ceiling and saw in the dim reflection that the other couple had left.

"Sorry, I was just thinking. I was trying to be creative." Wendy smirked at me and I started planning our fourth date.

"Okay, let's hear what you've got then."

"Alright. What if the waiter here was actually a spy. He drugged our food so he could control our minds and force us both to marry him. But, he doesn't know that we're also spies who've built up an immunity to mind control drugs." Wendy smiled and pointed her finger gun at me from across the table. "I love it. And then we pull out our cool spy weapons to fight him off. I've got a lipstick that shoots fireballs."

"And I've got a dart gun that paralyzes people. But wait, there are more spies," I stuck my head out of the booth to look around. "I think they could be anywhere. They're probably surrounding the restaurant right now so we can't escape." Wendy laughed and turned around to look for any potential spies at the tables around us. She looked back at me, and her glasses were out of place again, just slightly.

Wendy licked over her chapped lips and pushed her glasses back up on her nose. I imagined the spies surrounding the restaurant, waiting for us. There was the table over with a tall man in a baseball hat. He was a spy. The man at the counter waiting for his pick-up order, holding a wet briefcase, spy.

Outside the rain was falling softly and I hoped it would still be when we left so I could offer Wendy my umbrella. All around us there was the lit up college town, surrounded by the fields and farms. The streetlights only went so far before it would be the woods and the dark, country paths that were better left undisturbed. I reached over and squeezed Wendy's hand. She squeezed back.

"I think we're surrounded. We better sit here for a while and wait it out."

If There's a Ledge to Hang From

SeaPoint Cove was not actually a cove, but it was a point. Situated across three miles of a leveled off mountain, along the northern coast of California, a brand new Lifestyle Community was constructed. It consisted of a small neighborhood of single family homes, a main street of shops and restaurants, and a few basic amenities, like a school, a theater, and a library. What made SeaPoint Cove different from other exclusive, luxury living was their explicit promise that within 50 years the ocean levels would rise and everyone in the community would own pristine, private beachfront property.

The promise of a beautiful and exclusive beach within a lifetime was enough to get a few young families flocking up the mountain and into their new homes. One young couple, Sandy and David, used all the money they'd saved for their honeymoon on a downpayment for a house in row three out of five in the neighborhood. All of the homes were staggered row by row with large bay windows that faced out towards the beach, at least where the beach would be. For now, it faced the cliff. The cliff's edge jutted out a good quarter mile or so over the open air. SeaPoint Cove's Development Company had put up a railing right at the edge and built a large metal sign that said, "Boardwalk". All the townspeople would walk along their boardwalk and look out over their ocean. It was down there somewhere, about 8,000 feet, through the cloud bank and fog. Everyone insisted that if you walked all the way out to the very end, opened your arms, squeezed your eyes shut, and held your breath, you could hear the waves crashing down below.

Sandy and David settled into their new community fairly easily. Sandy got a job at the local library and David started working for SeaPoint Cove's Community Improvement Taskforce. It was a group of young residents who wanted to make the most of their neighborhood and really put SeaPoint Cove on the map. Their first order of business was constructing a temporary beach. Just because the real thing would take a little while didn't mean they couldn't enjoy all the activities that came with living in an oceanside town. Thirty tons of sand were airlifted in and spread around the area just south of the cliff's edge so people could still enjoy the view while they sun bathed or made sandcastles. They installed volleyball nets, lounge chairs, and a surfboard rental. The sand was contained mostly through a clever netting system underneath, and a small crew was employed to regularly sweep the edges of the beach back into order. Being so high up, windstorms were frequent. After the third volleyball net was blown right off the mountain, the Taskforce elected to stop installing new ones. They began drafting plans for a tennis court instead.

SeaPoint Cove aimed to provide an authentic, beach-town life from the scenery all the way to the shopping district. Their Main Street was lined with garlands of colorful flags and miniature lighthouse statues between the shops and restaurants. Only a few were open now, but they had plans to open more as residents continued moving in. For now, there was a seafood restaurant that boasted excellent clam chowder from fresh, airdropped clams and a sandwich shack. There was a corner store that sold swimsuits and snorkels, an old-fashioned candy shop, and a souvenir shop that sold home decor along with shirts and snowglobes. Sandy and David obtained most of their decorations from this shop. Their favorite piece was a wire and plaster seagull statue wearing sunglasses and holding an ice cream cone in one wing.

Sandy and David embraced their daily routine with dedication and enthusiasm. In the mornings, they would have breakfast and walk to work together. David was working on plans for a community center building and Sandy was teaching art classes and other programs for the sparse library patrons. When they returned home in the evening, they would cook and eat dinner together in their small, yellow kitchen. After dinner, they would go on a walk. Hand in hand, Sandy and David would circle the town and walk all the way out to the edge of the boardwalk. There, they would open their arms, close their eyes, hold their breath, and listen for the waves down below.

Sandy would let the wind whip back her hair and rush in her ears. She was sure the ocean was there, somewhere below. She would peek her eyes open while David's remained closed. All she could see were stars and the distant lights of town behind her. Sometimes she would sit in the grass, even dangle her feet off the cliff's edge in an attempt to get closer. She longed to feel the ocean spray on her fingers, hear a real seagull, anything that would tell her it was coming. All she ever got was wind.

Every so often, SeaPoint Cove would get tourists. People from small towns further down the mountain and the surrounding area would drive up to see what the fuss was about. Most of them would quickly leave, declining the townspeople's smiling offers of saltwater taffy and guided tours. SeaPoint Cove's Development Company decided the town could be more colorful, more inviting to tourists and potential homebuyers. Murals were commissioned on almost every building on Main Street and a speaker system was installed to play a soundscape of ocean waves and bird calls 14 hours a day. Trucks of delicate, beautiful flowers were brought in for residents to add to their yards. Many of the flowers died after a couple of weeks, not the right varieties equipped for the cold and windy mountain air. There were plans in the works to hire artists to construct fake flowers out of cloth and wire to replace them, possibly even open a flower shop.

One night, almost half a year into living in their new home, David noticed a dip in their kitchen floor. There was a hole, perfectly round, and about the size of his palm. Carefully, he shined a flashlight into the hole, but couldn't see anything. David found that odd, surely underneath the floor was the cement foundation all the homes were built on. Under that, he supposed there was just dirt. This was as if someone had taken a perfect, cookie-cutter chunk right out of the ground. David didn't want to be late for work, so he resolved to talk with Sandy about it later.

David wondered if the hole had been his imagination, too much caffeine from the coffee house that had opened with the newest influx of families. But when he and Sandy returned home that evening, the hole had grown to almost a foot in diameter. Still perfectly round, and perfectly dark. Sandy looked closer, sticking her hand carefully into the hole and searching for an edge, or wires, anything really. She tried lighting a match, but as soon as it went into the hole, all the light was gone. David put in a call to the Development Company's Resident Satisfaction Division, surely a hole like this spoke to greater structural issues and safety concerns. The company said they would send someone over.

The repair people came and inspected the hole. They stuck a rope with an industrial light attached inside and after they lost both the light and ran out of rope, they said they would have to come back the following week. The couple was advised to monitor the hole but to go on with life as normal. They would be back to patch it up before they knew it. Over the next week, the hole grew to about three feet in diameter and took up the center of their kitchen. Sandy made a joke about tossing their food scraps in it, but David had been annoyed with the situation ever since he had dropped his keys inside by accident. The repair team called back a few days later and said that with the high demand of building projects going on, it would take them a little longer to fix the hole and thanked them for their patience.

Word spread fast around town about the couple's mysterious hole in the floor. Neighbors started coming by, offering pitchers of lemonade and peach cobblers in order to glimpse a peek. David and his team with the Community Improvement Taskforce drafted a list of possible fixes that included nailing boards of wood across it or throwing a large rug on top of it. David tried both of these, but each time the hole spread until the obstruction was sucked inside. The hole was just over five feet in diameter now. Sandy kept testing the hole as well, shining different lights inside and even shouting out 'Hello' to see if there was a response. When she was close to the edge of the hole, she swore there was a light breeze, like a wind current gently pulling her inward.

When she told her coworkers about the hole, her friend Marta pulled her aside and asked if she could come by to see it. Sandy didn't see any harm and invited her over for lunch. Marta showed up that weekend with a pasta salad and a sealed envelope. She explained how she had lost her husband before moving to SeaPoint Cove and thought it might be nice to write him a letter. It had been sitting on her dresser at home for weeks and she wondered if she could drop it into the hole. Sandy let her, of course, and together they watched as the white envelope disappeared swiftly into the darkness. Afterwards, they ate the pasta salad and Marta said she felt like a weight had been lifted.

After Marta's visit, more people started showing up with things they wanted to throw into the hole. It was cathartic, it seemed, to toss something away into the unknown. Sandy tossed something away too. While David worked late, developing plans on a new snow cone stand to replace the one blown off the mountain, she had drawn a picture. It was of the beach she grew up down the street from, back in Michigan. She drew the dune grass and the hot, squishy sand filled with little shells and pebbles. She drew the waves, rolling in and lapping at the shore. Sandy let her picture go and watched it get eaten by the floor.

It turned out that the hole in Sandy and David's kitchen floor was the best attraction SeaPoint Cove had to offer. After Shirley, one of the other librarians, had told her grandson about the hole, he drove up with a group of his friends from Santa Barbara to try dropping things in and investigate. They made a video about 'The Bottomless Pit', posted it online, and suddenly cars filled with curious people started showing up in SeaPoint Cove. Tourists lined up to see the hole, take a picture, and toss something inside. Sandy and David were unsure at first about all the people coming into their home, but the traffic was good for the town's development, and all the extra revenue spent at the shops was going to fund a roller-skating rink.

For weeks, all day long, people would come and ring the couple's doorbell. They both had to take time off work to properly manage the flow of traffic. Families with kids would take pictures posing in front of the hole. The bravest would take pictures holding their children up and over the hole. One family had a few kids, each with something to throw inside. The youngest child, a small boy clutching a teddy bear, seemed hesitant to let it go. He leaned over, trying to see where it would land, if the hole really was as bottomless as it seemed. He leaned and leaned and leaned and leaned.

After the boy and his bear, people stopped coming to SeaPoint Cove. It was mainly because Sandy and David stopped answering the doorbell. The rescue crew had left, packing up their gear and lanterns with sad shakes of their heads, too afraid to venture inside after their ropes and cameras showed nothing but darkness. The crowds outside eventually dispersed. David put in regular calls all week to the Development Company, trying to get someone to come and fix their floor. Sandy went back to work and smiled as she shelved books, but she took longer lunch breaks alone outside. Her and David still ate dinner together, but they did so in the living room instead of the kitchen. They still took evening walks too, but they didn't talk. They walked a distance apart from each other, hands stuffed in coat pockets and their eyes fixed on the flat, gray horizon.

Finally, David got a call back, but it wasn't from the repair people, it was the president of SeaPoint Cove's Development Team calling with an offer. He wanted to buy their house. It was a tragedy, he insisted, a real tragedy what happened. He wanted to take the house off their hands, remove any emotional burdens for them. SeaPoint Cove planned to convert the house and its Bottomless Pit into a landmark. They would put up a memorial for that family, of course, but such an amazing site deserved to be witnessed. In exchange, SeaPoint Cove would provide them with a new house. He told David they had been developing a new community, a premiere neighborhood of SeaPoint Cove with larger, more modern family homes. They were being built just a couple miles East of town. Plans were being drawn for a helicopter landing pad and a yacht marina once they finished leveling off the land. David thanked the man and told him they would start packing immediately. The man informed David the houses were almost finished, but to hold off packing for a few days until they were painted and ready to move in.

David went home to tell Sandy about the new house, but she wasn't there. She wasn't at the library or the sandwich shack either. He found her out on the boardwalk, all the way at the cliff's edge where the wind had blown chunks of earth off the cliff and into the sea below. The edge was narrower now, sharper too. Sandy was standing with her arms open, breath held, and eyes wide open. David took her hand in his and walked them back. He didn't let go as they walked through town together. The speakers were acting up again, static clipping in over the endless loop of wave sounds and seagull calls. They walked together, hand in hand, and David promised the new house would be a new start.

Sandy and David split a bowl of clam chowder that evening and started planning how they would decorate a bigger house.

A few days passed and David hadn't heard anything more from the Development Company. Someone had come by to inspect their current home and install a safety rope, carpeted path, and a ticket booth around the hole. Sandy and David went to work, ate their dinner in the living room, and waited for the phone to ring. They had packed most of the house away already and were quickly growing restless. The weather took an unusually rough turn. Rain and hail pounded down on SeaPoint Cove, wrecking yard ornaments and wreaking havoc on their artificial beach. Many of the building's roofs had leaks and Sandy was spending the day putting proactive covers over all the library shelves. David was home, all community improvement projects on hold until the storms passed. With nothing else to do, he put on his rain boots and coat to take a walk.

David walked East instead of through town, towards the thick and untouched woods outside of their picket fences and speaker systems. He was looking for SeaPoint Cove's new community project. Just a quick look. Maybe if the house seemed close enough to being done, David could call and inform the company they would move in as is. Afterall, he and Sandy could handle some of the finishing themselves.

David walked further into the woods that still claimed most of the mountain. He walked through tall grass, past lush ferns and wildflowers. He walked along a rushing stream filled with sparkling river rocks and jumping frogs. David felt lucky to live in such a place. Maybe they could install a zipline here over the stream.

Eventually, he came out of the woods at a clearing filled with beautiful houses. There were about eight of them, with grand, curved front doors and beautiful iron banisters. The windows were large and framed with flower boxes. Many of the homes had Victorian style torrents and sunrooms while a couple others were more modern and geometric in design. David walked closer, wondering which house would be theirs, but as he got closer, something felt off. The house fronts were so flat, the windows didn't reflect any light, and as the rain hit them they swayed. David realized they were *only* fronts. Each beautiful house was painted on large, nailed together pieces of wood and propped up in the clearing. The houses here weren't close to being finished at all. They didn't even exist.

David walked up to the wooden fronts and saw how the paint was haphazardly slapped onto the wood. Up close, they were a mess of dirt and jagged nails. He kicked the side of one, hard. He kicked it again and the wood shuddered all the way up to the top where a piece fell loose, falling into the grass. David jumped back. He watched the painted facade get battered by the storm, swaying and creaking where it stood. Some of the paint was starting to wash off, dripping down the wood and nails into muddy puddles where it sunk into the damp earth below.

When Sandy got home from work, she was alone. The storm was in full swing, pelting almost sideways against the windows. She lit a lamp and crept around the hole in the floor to make something for dinner. While she chopped peppers and onions, Sandy heard dripping from somewhere in the house. She grabbed a bowl and a few dishtowels and went in search of the leak. Sandy walked through the whole house and couldn't find anything, ending up back in the kitchen, finally noticing where the sound was coming from. The hole in the floor.

Sure enough, from the darkness Sandy could hear a faint dripping sound. For the first time in weeks, she let herself look inside the hole. Sandy sat at its edge and leaned over, still seeing nothing. She leaned further, her hair dangling into the dark. She felt the same breeze as before, similar to a drafty cave. She stuck an arm in and wiggled it around, trying to find where the drip was coming from, but still couldn't see a thing. Sandy laid on the ground on her stomach. She crawled, reached her arms and head out over the hole, and closed her eyes. She swore she felt a drop of water hit her finger when the sounds of the front door opening prompted her to pull herself back up.

David walked in soaking wet and holding a single piece of plywood in his hand. He set it on the table and laughed, a little out of breath, and wiped a wet hand across his forehead. Sandy asked him if it was time to go.

Together, they packed their remaining clothes and belongings into the final moving boxes. They left the larger furniture and stacked their boxes into the car they had driven up the mountain in. Sandy pulled her seagull statue out of the lawn and they added it to the backseat of their car. None of their neighbors came out to wave goodbye, they might not have even noticed they were leaving. Sandy and David drove out of SeaPoint Cove and back down the mountain, winding around narrow roads bordered by tall trees and wildflowers. When they finally reached the base a couple hours later the rain had stopped. They drove down a long highway with the ocean right beside them. Waves crashed up onto the beach and Sandy rolled down her window to hear them better.

Buried in the Sleep

The detectives coming meant that we had to shut down the line for almost three full hours. It was probably the longest we'd all stood around since the big blackout back in 2003 when that storm had rolled through and nearly knocked the old supermarket clear off its foundation. No one ever knows what to do when the line's not running. You can't really talk because your ears keep on ringing like nothing was even turned off. Then, just as they start to adjust, you hear the clucking.

We keep the chickens in a separate building out back. They're fed through the line and come out dead, clean, and ready to be cooked or packed up. It's all designed in a way that's supposed to stop the birds from getting scared, but they know what's happening. They're not stupid. It's not unusual for a few chickens here and there to break out, go running out into the woods or something. You see them out there, mostly just carcasses left by the foxes or coyotes. But every now and then you see a live one, just running around all puffed up like it's daring you to try something. I steer clear of them, figure there's enough chicken karma stacked against me already.

When the detectives showed up Mr. Peterson ran out to meet them right away. He was dressed extra nice, in his light blue suit he usually reserved for lawyers and health inspectors, with his shiny brown dress shoes that he wore every day, even in the snow. I always imagine he had a closet filled with brown dress shoes all in neat rows with a polishing cloth hanging right beside them.

He was a short man with a thick neck, thicker arms, and a mop of curly, dark hair he kept slicked back with gel. Never without rings, about one on every finger, all made of heavy gold.

Mr. Peterson ushered the detectives upstairs as soon as they arrived. His office was there, away from all the noise. They were inside for a while before the alarms went off, signaling the line powering down. Elva was standing next to me when everything turned off. She turned to me with raised eyebrows, mouthing out *what the hell*. I shrugged back at her.

We stood around for a while, rocking on our heels until the two detectives came back downstairs and split up. I tried not to look too interested in where they were going. The taller one was a man with thick glasses and a long, well-groomed beard, headed off towards the packaging department in the next building. The second detective was a bit scrawny looking with wispy blonde hair and a suit jacket too big for him. He headed right for me and Elva.

"Ma'am," he murmured politely as he reached us. I watched his lips move but barely heard the greeting.

"Son, you'll have to speak up if you want anyone to hear you in here," I shouted at him.

"Ma'am, if you have a minute I'd like to—" his voice cut out as the ringing in my ear rose. I patted him on the shoulder and motioned for him to swap places with me, putting him to my left.

"My hearing isn't so great in my right ear, what were you saying, now?"

"I'd like to talk to you about Ginny Lewis if you have a minute," he yelled. The man's voice was deeper than you'd think looking at him, raspy, like he'd just gotten over being sick or something.

"I suppose. What's all this about Ginny?"

"When was the last time you saw Miss Lewis?"

"It must have been last week some time. The girl worked with me and Elva," I waved towards her. "She was real young, the young ones don't usually stick around long here. I wasn't too surprised she stopped coming."

73

"Are you sure you saw her last week?" the man asked.

"Must have, she came in on time, not like some of these slackers they hire. She was fine, just young. Why?"

"We believe Ginny Lewis is missing." I laughed a bit at that. The detective looked surprised.

"You don't think so?" he frowned.

"I think she'll send us a postcard when she reaches Vegas."

"Did she ever say anything like that? Mention any plans?"

"No, we didn't talk much," Elva chimed in. "Mr. Peterson probably knows the most out of any of us, he was always coming down here during her break. He talked to her quite a few times, I believe." The man scribbled down notes on a pad of paper.

Elva winked at me, and I rolled my eyes, "Come on, now. You make it sound like he was fixed on her or something."

"Wasn't he?" she giggled.

I scoffed and turned back to the detective, "What's your name, sir?"

"Erik, ma'am. Detective Erik Dombrowski. You are?"

"Bernice McCabe, sir. Benny is just fine too."

"Elva Sandoval." He jotted our names down in his notebook. Elva excused herself to go smoke before the line turned back on. The detective stayed beside me, still writing. He had one of those fancy pens with the metal tops that clicked.

"So, Miss Lewis never said anything directly to you, but she spoke with Mr. Peterson a few times, is that correct?"

"I guess."

"How long have you worked here?"

"It'll be twenty-five years in the spring."

"Does Mr. Peterson talk to a lot of the employees here?"

"Not particularly."

"Does he talk to you?"

75

"Maybe if he'd caught me thirty years ago."

The detective's mouth twitched, "What role do you play here?"

"We inspect the birds. They come through those chutes," I pointed to the right, "and onto these belts. We make sure there aren't any stuck feathers left, then press this," I pointed again, "and that dome comes down to spray the birds. It gives them a final clean before they're sent over to be packaged as is or cooked." He didn't write any of that down, but I guess he was probably asking to be polite.

"Did Miss Lewis ever mention anybody to you? Someone she spent time with, or did you ever see her with anybody?"

"Not really. I didn't know her too well." Ginny didn't smoke so she never joined me and Elva on breaks. I could recall her sitting for lunch every day with a neatly packed sandwich and a soda. She played with her hair a lot and was always crossing and uncrossing her ankles like she could never get comfortable. She wore a necklace, which was against dress code, and kept it tucked into her shirt. I saw the charm once when it had come loose, a small heart covered in little crystals. A bit tacky if you ask me.

The detective's partner reappeared down the line and waved him over. The two of them talked together for a minute before exiting the factory without another glance. Mr. Peterson came out of his office after they left and stared at the doors. He tapped his hands against the metal railings making his rings clank like water pipes. I realized they sounded different than I thought they would, quieter. Eventually he went back into his office without a word and turned back on the line.

The sun was mostly down when I left work. It was getting dark earlier and earlier; we'd already had our rainy season and now with the temperature dropping, icy water was pooling up on the ground creating deep, muddy holes and flooding a bunch of the backroads I liked to take. Any sunlight from the day sunk deep into the mud and was forgotten, leaving nothing but fog rolling along the ground. It gave me the feeling that all the warmth was draining out of the world, but I tried not to let that thought get to me.

I stopped at Jax's Gas Station to fill up and grab a six pack. The boy behind the counter, Clark, was always around. He was a highschooler with short, spikey hair and too much cheap cologne on. He passed over my usual order with a smug smile before I could ask.

"Aren't you ever out seeing a movie or anything?" I asked. "Kids are supposed to go and cause trouble, not be working all the time." Clark laughed at me, showing off all his perfectly straight teeth.

"And miss the chance to see your beautiful face, Benny? I would never!"

"You better call me Mrs. McCabe or I'm going to start thinking you're sweet on me." He just winked and passed me back my change. Clark was a sweet boy.

"How've you been doing anyways, Benny?"

"Oh, I'm alright. There's nothing to fuss over."

"You still haven't heard from George?" he asked hesitantly.

"Psh," I clicked my tongue, "it's like I said, nothing to fuss over."

"I just gotta check on you. If you ever need help around the house or anything..."

"I'm not going anywhere anytime soon, sweetheart. Don't you worry about me." Clark carried my bag out to my car and I finished the short drive back home. I only lived a couple miles outside of town, not quite into the farmlands. George had wanted to do the whole thing: goats, chickens, and pigs or whatever. We never got around to getting a single animal even though he built a half-assed chicken coop.

My lot was about three in from the main road. The houses were spread out pretty far on this side of town with healthy stretches of backwoods between them all. Our house was bordered by trees on all sides, except for a wide dirt and gravel path that served as the driveway. I pulled in behind George's truck. He'd left it right in the center of the driveway.

I should sell the thing, but I guess I was keeping it around until it seemed okay to get rid of. I didn't want to do anything too fast. I'd drive it myself, but I never liked those pickup things, too big and too high off the ground for me. Riding in it with George had always made my knees hurt. Maybe Clark was looking for something to take to college. I'd give him a good deal if he wanted the stupid thing.

I could sell a lot of George's stuff. There was the riding mower I'd never use, a bunch of scrap metal cluttering up the garage, and the God-awful pool table down in the basement with all those beer bottles littering it. Collecting all the glass bottles scattered around, alone, would buy me a nice meal out with Elva. Our front porch was still covered in them; my back hurt too much this time of year to bend over and pick them all up, so I'd just shoved them into a corner. Maybe when the weather got a bit warmer I'd get around to it. I could fix up the place, plant some flower boxes or something.

It was warm inside. I had started cranking the heat when I left for work, to get the ancient radiators going by the time I got home. It gave the place a musty smell, but it was better than freezing. I grabbed a beer, put the rest in the fridge, and heated up a frozen meatloaf. I sat on the couch and ate, the only sound besides my fork scraping the plastic container was the wind hitting the chimes outside. When George and I had first moved in, I thought I'd miss having neighbors close by. I grew up on a crowded cul-de-sac, one of five kids. There would always be bike bells ringing, people talking, someone cooking outside. Out here, there was nobody but me. Most of the time, at least.

I swallowed back a yawn and stretched out my legs, listening to my hip crack. It was that time of the evening where my eyelids started drooping and my whole body became slow and sleepy. I turned on the TV, just some nature documentary that was going, some noise to keep me awake. There was no sense in trying to go to bed beforehand. I had to stay up until he was done. Sure enough, as soon as I picked up my knitting needles, I heard the first shuffle of steps outside.

The knocking was a loud and constant drum against the front door. I knew he'd never be able to break through it, but it didn't stop him from trying. He had put that door in himself, a solid wooden thing unlike the flimsy tin and screen one that had come with the house. I gripped my knitting needles tighter and turned up the television to drown it out. It didn't do any good to yell at him, and I sure as hell wasn't going to open the door. He'd knock until he was done. The door, the windows too, the walls, I swear I'd heard him on the roof before. I had put up heavy blinds that stayed shut all day and night so I wouldn't have to see his face peering in anymore, at least.

I just focused on my knitting. I couldn't make much, but I kept at it. The soothing motion of my circular needles working down in neat rows helped me keep my head. I didn't even jump much anymore when he really slammed on the walls. I had made coasters, table runners, basically anything I could do in a straight line. This one was going to be a scarf. If I could get through it without any knots, maybe I'd give it to Elva. The knocking continued in a steady, pounding rhythm until, abruptly, it stopped. After a minute of silence, I cracked my knuckles and set aside my knitting to shuffle off to bed. I had gotten used to never feeling fully rested.

In the bleary light of early morning, I made my coffee and left the house to find muddy footprints spread all across the porch. They stretched the full length to George's chair and back down the stairs. The steps showed a clear shoe heel and clumps of mud from worn down dress shoes. The steps continued to George's truck, circled around it, and went back into the woods across the yard. I stomped through some of them to get to my car. I didn't bother trying to scrub them away anymore. That was the thing about dirt, it was hard to get rid of. Once even a little gets on you, it's all over. No matter how much you clean, scrape, or shovel. Dirt never wants to let go.

I figured those detectives had been a one-time thing. They usually are in a place like this. People get hurt doing all sorts of crap, and they always send someone in a nice suit to check up afterwards. They never do much, just walk around the scene of the crime and then disappear. I remember after Caleb Mitchells got his arm shredded on the line, they had sent someone from the insurance company. He had worn a beige suit and absolutely refused to walk anywhere close to where Caleb had been injured. He had his assistant with him, a shorter man in khakis and a tucked in dress shirt, go up to the machine and poke around for him. Caleb still hasn't gotten his check from that mess.

So, I was surprised when that same detective from yesterday appeared beside me as I was walking in from the parking lot. I stopped short and he turned, giving me a slight wave.

"Ma'am," he greeted cordially.

"Morning," I replied automatically. "Where's your partner at?"

"On other business, I thought I'd come back here today. Maybe I'll see you around, Benny," the detective held the front door open for me and waved me through, smiling.

"I'm afraid I don't remember your name," I said.

"Erik, ma'am. Or detective Dombrowski if you'd please," he winked at me.

"Erik, you better watch those nice shoes in here. Chicken blood tends to stain." He coughed and made a face.

"Duly noted," he said. I walked by him without a goodbye, "Have a nice day, Benny," he shouted after me. I didn't turn back. I hung up my coat and hurried back to my station. It was better, in a place like this, not to draw unnecessary attention. I didn't need to see what happened once Mr. Peterson caught wind of that man snooping around again. Something about those detectives made him twitchier than the last time the regional manager came for a meeting unannounced.

I didn't get what the big deal was. Maybe our coops weren't up to every code in the books. Maybe the people working here weren't the perfect example of food-grade sanitation either, but shit, it was just chicken packing. Not like we're handling anything fancy. People get what they pay for and Barley and Brown Chickens are sold proudly at just about every gas station from here to Reno. If that man wanted to traipse through chicken poop all day, I wasn't going to go out there and stop him. Maybe a chicken bite would do him some good.

It was getting too cold to stand around outside for long, but I still wanted a smoke. Elva waved me off, opting to stay inside to eat during our break. I was almost finished with my second cigarette when I saw the detective walking back from the chicken coops.

"What the hell," I muttered under my breath. He must have spent the whole morning wandering around out there, what on earth for? I watched him stumble around and wave to someone, then the other detective walked out of the woods. He was more bundled up, with a coat and gloves. His boots and the knees of his pants were caked with mud. He faced away from me, waving his arms about something like he was angry. Detective Erik looked around and caught my eye. He waved. I coughed around my cigarette. By the time I got my hand up to wave back he was already walking over, leaving his partner behind.

"Detective," I croaked out to him when he was in earshot. "You're still poking around here?"

"Just a bit," he chuckled.

"I'm catching a cold just looking at you. Don't you have a warmer coat?" He looked over what he was wearing and shrugged. "Well, good luck I guess. I've got to head back in."

"Of course, but before you go, just one thing?" I rolled my eyes but waited for him to continue. "Did you ever see Ginny Lewis talking with anyone? Or ever hear anyone talking about her? Someone you recognized, or maybe not?"

"I don't hear much of anything in there. It's not really the type of place where you can gossip all day. Look, we all come in, do our work, and go home. It's hard work and long hours with machines knocking around your eardrums all day. Nobody sticks around here if they've got other options. These young ladies don't want to ruin their shoulders or their nails doing this forever. They come to make some money, then they move on to something else. Nothing more to it than that."

"So you've noticed a few women disappear from here?" Erik's partner asked. He had walked over as well and was jotting down something in a notebook similar to Erik's.

"Not *disappear*. Christ," I stomped out the butt of my cigarette, "Look, I don't keep a tally of everyone who comes and goes. People just go off sometimes. They get married, get pregnant, or just get a different job somewhere else. Shit! We're about three days to California, detective. I keep saying it and ya'll don't hear me. Nobody sticks around here unless they have to."

"You don't find it strange she never mentioned moving?" the partner countered immediately, unfazed by my outburst.

"It doesn't take a genius to figure out. Somebody doesn't show up for work, after a week or two, there's someone new."

"And has Mr. Peterson ever taken a liking to anyone else?" Erik asked. I rolled my eyes.

"Mr. Peterson takes a liking to anything young with curly hair and lipstick. Hell, if some of our chickens had longer legs I'm sure he'd be all over them too!" Erik snorted and his partner gave him a disapproving look. "It doesn't mean a thing is all I'm saying."

"And are these women who have also left town abruptly?" the partner asked.

"I don't know. What do I look like, the bookkeeper? I know I wouldn't want to stick around if I saw what that man looked like after hours. Now excuse me, I've got to get back to it, boys."

86

"Have a good day, Benny," Erik replied, smiling. I thought I saw his partner elbow him out of the corner of my eye after I had turned back to the factory. I washed up quickly and nearly ran back to my station.

Mr. Peterson was standing by the line when I returned.

"You're seven minutes late," he shouted over the roar of machinery. I waved my hands behind me,

"Those detectives wouldn't let me go," I shouted back. "Nosy buggers." He crossed his arms across his chest.

"What do they want with you?"

I threw my hands up, "Nothing! It's all just nonsense if you ask me." He nodded curtly and walked off without another word.

"That blonde detective sure is chatty with you," Elva shouted at me, wiggling her eyebrows under her hair net. I flipped her off and pulled on my work gear. Mr. Peterson didn't look back. He stomped up the stairs to his office with an unusual vigor. His regular slacks rustled against his shiny dress shoes, the same ones he wore every day. Except, today there was a little bit of mud stuck to the backs of his heels.

Getting mud on your shoes was an everyday event around here. It was always either muddy or dusty, sometimes both at the same time. The dirt here never stayed where it was supposed to. Landslides were common too, they came with long periods of rain overflowing the banks they had once tried to redirect to feed into reservoirs. The earth was too easy to move around if you ask me. Things should stay where you leave them, like roots and houses. But if you move around the dirt, it starts fighting back. Dirt could unlock all kinds of things, like rings once lost or car keys. Too many things, like shoe prints leading out into the woods or muddy boot prints all over a porch—dirt didn't keep as many secrets as it should.

Mr. Peterson never came to work dirty. He seemed to think being clean separated him from the rest of us. His shiny belts and equally polished hair, always gleaming in the dim light right along with his rings. I laughed a little to myself, thinking about how he didn't even know he'd stepped in a puddle and wouldn't figure it out until he got back home.

I thought back to Erik and that other detective, this was probably the sort of thing they'd spend hours poring over. Detectives like to pick apart little things like that, don't they? What you've got on, how you talk, if your teeth are a little crooked. Nosy buggers. George always picked on little things like that too. He cared if people were put together right or not. He was always fussing over me and the dirt under my fingernails. I couldn't stand people who fussed. Ginny had always seemed fussy too. She wore her blonde hair braided down her back, a few curls coming loose around her eyes as the day went on. She wore makeup which would sweat down her face all morning, then she'd go and fix it, only to have it sweat right off again.

Poor girl, wherever she was. She probably got knocked up and split. Whatever happened to her, that girl's family must have made a real racket to have these two yahoos poking and prodding everywhere. I hoped they never found her. I hoped wherever she'd run off to, it was all worth it and she was happy. Wouldn't that be nice?

After work, I stopped by the gas station again to grab some groceries, mostly canned soup, and more cigarettes. Clark added in a free scratch off and slid it over to me with an offer to help me carry things out to my car.

"My back's not broken yet, gotta keep in shape as long as I can," I replied.

"Benny, you know I'm available to help. Even just to shovel for you when it snows. I'm just saying, you can ask me for anything."

"That's a very sweet offer. Just an excuse to snoop around my house, I'm sure."

"You don't know that," he laughed. "Really though, don't be afraid to ask for help. You don't have to be out there alone."

I smiled all the way back to my car. There were a few good parts to sticking around here, I suppose. People knew me. Not too many that someone would come knocking unexpectedly, but just enough that I didn't have to worry about rotting down to my bones on the couch. Sometimes it seemed like I should just close my eyes, sink back into the cushions, and get it over with sooner than later. It wouldn't have to be loud or drawn-out. Too many people spent too much time dying. When my mother went, she dropped to the living room floor like a lightswitch went off. That's what I want. No time to be scared of something you don't see coming.

I had just started on my second beer and some canned ravioli, when it started that evening. The knocks sounded a bit different. It was too early, and these were softer, more spaced out. It took me a minute to put together that there was somebody at the door. I hurried up from the couch and undid all the locks, cursing under my breath. Standing outside was Detective Erik.

"Apologies Ma'am, I saw your lights on and could use a bit of assistance."

"Detective?" I asked, bewildered. He blinked a couple times and squinted at me.

"Benny?" he asked back. "You live here?"

"You've got to be kidding me. I hope you're not here to ask me more questions about Ginny Lewis, I was just finishing dinner."

"No, no ma'am," he stuttered out loudly, waving his hands wildly in front of him. "I'm terribly sorry, I was actually hoping to use a phone. My car got stuck in the mud about half a mile back and your house was the first one I saw with any lights on. I managed to get the back of the car out, but not without popping the tire." Erik's shoes and the bottoms of his pants were caked in mud.

Behind him, the sky was a dusty purple, quickly fading into black. It was only a matter of time until he'd be coming, but I couldn't turn Erik away without incurring any questions either. I clicked my tongue behind my teeth, "Come on in, then. Just make it fast. And roll up your pants, I don't want you dripping on my carpet."

He stepped around me and into the house. I could see his eyes shift to look around my living room. I could only imagine what he saw. Scratched up wooden floors and dirty green carpet littered with cigarette burns. Wallpaper that had seen better days and empty beer bottles in the sink. An overfilled trash can. And of course, everything from the wall clock to the windows draped in half-assed knitted yarn.

"Should I take my shoes off?" he asked. I gave him a flat look and he started undoing the muddy laces.

"Leave them by the door," I replied. "Wash your hands in the kitchen, the phone is on the wall. Can I get you anything to drink?" He looked me over for a minute, like he was debating asking something else. He was wearing green and yellow striped socks which looked out of place against his gray, monochrome outfit. In his socks and muddy, rolled up pants he followed me obediently over to the sink where he washed the dirt from his hands with my dish soap. He toweled them off and I pointed to the phone.

"Thank you, Benny," he said softly. I stood rigid with my arms folded while he dialed a number and waited. He dialed again. And a third time.

"You can always try the tire shop up on fifth and western, they have an after-hours number I can dig out of my book for you."

"If you could, I would appreciate it," Erik replied. "Is this whole place immune to cell service?"

"It gets spotty farther from downtown. Your partner isn't picking up?" I pulled my phone book out of its drawer with all my takeout menus and different scraps of coupons. I pointed to the number, "Here you go. His name's Dan but his son might answer. His kid is also named Dan though so I guess it doesn't matter too much," I trailed off. "Anyways, someone should at least answer," I turned away from Erik and busied myself with rustling through the rest of the papers in that drawer while he talked on the phone. Most of this stuff was in George's illegible, crap handwriting. I crumpled a bunch of it into a ball and threw it into the trash. The sun had to be fully gone by now. I balled my hands into fists to keep them from shaking. Finally, Erik set down the phone and stepped back.

"Thanks again, I think I can head out soon to go meet him by the car. He said he'd bring me a spare and that should last until I can get a new tire."

"You didn't have a spare already?"

"I don't think so?" he stared at the floor.

"Did you check?"

"Not exactly." He sighed, "Sorry again to bother you, I'm not used to being out on all these dirt roads. I'm glad I ran into you though." I tried to keep the grimace off my face and instead focused on squeezing my hands together. Time was running out.

"Well, glad I could offer you a phone at least. You better head back now. It gets dark quick around here." I was barely paying attention as I waved Erik back towards the front door. He looked right past me towards the back windows and I felt my heart jump into my throat.

"You have a gun," he said simply.

"What?"

"A gun," he repeated. He pointed to the wall that held George's shotgun. Of course, the stupid detective cared about that stupid gun.

"So? Everybody around here has a gun."

"Do you hunt?"

"No. My husband does. Did, I mean. Rabbits mostly. Sometimes deer. He was never a very good shot." George had got the gun at a show, down in Oklahoma before we even got married. He used to keep it in the bedroom at our first place and shine it once a week. I could never get the stains from the polish fully out of the sheets.

"I'm sorry for your loss," Erik said quietly.

"Don't be," I snapped. "Idiot wanted to run off for years. I'm sure he's doing something worthwhile," I chewed on my lip. "Anyways, you should head out and get back to your car. You've got lots to do, I'm sure. It's hard work looking for people who don't want to be found." Erik followed me to the door this time. I noticed my hands were shaking again and I hid them behind my back.

"You make a lot of assumptions about Ginny for someone who claims to have not talked to her much," Erik said. "What makes you so sure she ran off?"

"I'm good at reading people I guess."

"I think they have a word for that—"

"Intelligence?"

"Projecting," he laughed. I snorted in reply. "We found her car, you know," Erik continued, still standing in front of the closed door. I could almost feel the clock tick vibrating in my good ear, marking the seconds as they passed.

"Oh, yeah?" I croaked out.

"It was parked in her building lot. Keys in her apartment. Her roommate said she had been leaving at night pretty frequently and assumed she was seeing someone but didn't know who."

"Maybe they took off together, then."

"Do you really believe that?" Erik scoffed.

"I believe that if people don't want to be found then they won't be."

"And what if they aren't hiding?"

"Better to leave well enough alone. None of my business." Moonlight was creeping in around the slats of my blinds. He would be here any minute. I reached behind Erik, "Anyways, I've got to get back to it." I unlocked the door. "Have a good night, now."

He still didn't move.

"Tell me one thing first, before I go," he insisted. I raised an eyebrow at him. He waved his hands around the room, "What's with all the yarn?"

"Everybody's got a hobby. Are you going to tell me you do interior design when you're not hunting down girls?" Erik's brow creased.

"You really believe that Ginny Lewis left town of her own accord."

"I keep saying so."

"Why? Because it's what you would do?"

"I'm still here, aren't I?" I crossed my arms across my chest. We stared at each other for a moment until there was a loud knock at the back door. I jumped back. Erik turned.

"Are you expecting company?" he asked.

"It's just the wind. Old house, you know?" I rushed out. Another knock.

"Are you sure?"

"Oh yeah, that happens all the time." There were shuffling steps around the side of the house. I coughed to cover the worst of the noise. "Anyways, have a pleasant night now, detective!" I waved him forward again and he continued to ignore me, lingering in front of the closed door.

"Here, let me give you my card. You can give me a call sometime if you ever think of anything else Ginny might have mentioned."

"Sure. Thanks." He handed the card over. Erik finally opened the door, and I followed him onto the porch, keeping one hand on the doorknob. My front yard was nearly pitch dark, the only light coming from inside my house and the moon's faint glow cast across the lawn. At the edge, right in between the trees, he was waiting.

Dripping dirt fell from George's outstretched arms. A few of his fingers were bent back and faintly twitching. The chunk of his head that was missing from where I had taken it out with his shotgun had gotten larger, like something had nibbled at the ridge of the wound. His shirt was ripped from where I had to drag him by the sleeves outside. He was covered in mud and almost invisible in the dark. Dim moonlight reflected off his cloudy, dead eyes. He stood perfectly still.

"Ah geez, did I track all this up?" Erik was looking at the fresh muddy footprints going up the stairs.

"Not you, probably my mailman. Don't worry about it," I whispered. Out across the yard, George shifted his weight and Erik's head snapped up to meet his eyes.

"Jesus!" he stepped back. Erik put his arm out in front of me. I forced a laugh to bubble out past my clenched teeth.

"What is it? Oh, that thing? That's just a scarecrow." Erik didn't take his eyes off of George. "Come on, detective. Surely you've seen one before, it's all paint and straw."

"It just moved!"

"Trick of the shadows. It gets the job done." Erik stared at George, and I held my breath. George remained still except for the mud still dripping off of him. Erik laughed and ran a hand up through his hair.

"Geez! That thing nearly had me reaching for my gun." George's glazed over eyes were fixed on me. His finger twitched again. I exhaled slowly,

"Well, goodnight detective," I spoke quietly, never moving my eyes away from George. "I've got to head back in. Good luck with your car."

"Goodnight Benny, thank you again. Remember, give me a call, anytime. For anything, really." I nodded and waved him off. Erik walked back the way he came, turning once more to wave and then disappearing down the driveway, away from George.

I stayed out on the porch, gripping my railing tight in one hand with the other still stretched behind me to keep a hold of the door. George stayed put.

"What do you want?" I shouted at him. "Asshole!" His eyes blinked once and his whole body rippled like the view out of a window in the rain. I backed into the house and slammed the door shut. Sure enough, a large smack hit the door just a few moments later.

He banged on the door hard enough to make the wood shake and my blinds rattle. It was like he was waiting for me to be alone again. I always suspected George came sniffing back around here just to irritate me. He always did like to try and scare me, got some sick satisfaction out of watching me squirm.

The first time I'd seen his face in the window, about two weeks after burying him, I'd thought it was guilt. Not that I felt any, but I figured maybe my subconscious was taking on a mind of its own. He had looked about the same then, a little gray in the face, and the side of his head a puss-filled, festering wound. He stood there peering in with an expression I'd seen a million times. The one that said, *what the hell, Benny?* and usually came before something bad happened. I'd put it together when the banging started. His face was still in the window, but the banging on the front door was too far away. I'd rushed over and double locked the door, pulled all my blinds shut, and sat up all night with the shotgun until he had gone away with the rising sun.

I don't think he's a zombie or anything like that. He's gotten droopier over time and some of the flesh around his hands and face was starting to come off. One eye is looking pretty worse for wear as well, sitting loose in his rotting skull. He shifts around and flickers more like a ghost, though; I don't know if he could hurt me or not. I'm not going to take any chances.

I figure I just have to outlast him. George will keep on deteriorating, and the worms will finish him off eventually. It's getting colder outside, pretty soon the earth will freeze over for the winter. I'm holding out hope that the dirt will keep him better once it's all solid. Maybe then I could try and get some more sleep.

A cold snap set in overnight, so I took the bus to work. My car never started well in the cold. Detective Erik wasn't at the factory and neither was his partner. Work grinded along as usual, not a single bird out of place. Elva and I smoked together on our break.

"Do you think they'll find her?" Elva asked me. "Ginny, I mean." I shrugged and exhaled. The chickens were clucking up a storm back in their coops, and I watched the tree-line, half expecting Erik or his partner to come stumbling out. They never did. Mr. Peterson paced along the upper floor of his office all afternoon. His shoes were freshly polished and perfectly clean.

It was cold enough to numb my face as I walked from the bus stop after work. Good thing Erik hadn't gotten his car stuck in weather like this, he'd have frozen in that silly trench coat he wore. I was just about freezing in my parka with my hands all balled up in my pockets.

Almost a quarter mile to home and instead of going straight along the road, I turned into the woods and headed West, careful not to step anywhere too muddy.

A mile or so in, then a little to the right, not too close to the river or any property lines. Just empty trees with no good hunting, not belonging to anybody. It was an area that got passed over year after year for being overgrown and too much of a hassle to do anything with.

I left him right beside a mossy rock with some loose sticks thrown around for good measure. The dirt was flat and patted down; that was my one mistake. It was too even looking, but now that the weeds had some time to regrow, it looked okay. I was probably standing right over his legs.

When I buried George, he hadn't wanted to go down. I'd sat there for hours, shoveling dirt over his stubborn head and one arm that had remained uncovered, almost like he was waving to me. I got him packed in eventually though. I stomped the dirt under my boot and felt the give. Still a little squishy, not quite frozen through yet.

"Anybody home?" I called quietly. I didn't expect much of a response. Either George was too frozen in there to get out again or he was already at the house causing a racket. I don't actually know what temperature it takes to freeze a ghost, especially a stubborn one. I waited around for a few minutes but didn't hear anything aside from the wind. I rubbed my hands over my face to keep the blood flowing and left. Walking back home, I looped around to one edge of a neighboring lot before making my way along the main road home. Last thing I needed to do was leave fresh prints in the mud, straight to him, especially while Erik and his partner were still probably poking around. A few yards down I heard a rustle in the bushes beside me. I stopped walking.

"George?" I whispered out into the dark. There was a muffled chirping and another rustle. I jumped back, just as a chicken came bursting out onto my path. It stumbled around before plopping itself down into the dirt. It was definitely one from the factory. It still had the tag tied around part of its wing. It was dirty and some of its feathers were hanging off at weird angles. The chicken looked at me and squawked.

"What are you doing out here then?" I asked. The chicken ignored me, continuing to scoot around in the dirt. It raised its head and stared at me for a moment before fluffing up its wings. Stuck around its leg was a dirty chain that had gotten wrapped around its foot and was squeezing the skin. The chicken squawked again. I bent forward to get a closer look, careful not to stick my important bits too close to its mouth. The chain was thin and had a single heart charm attached to it, all caked in mud. I reached out slowly, careful not to get bitten, and unknotted the chain. As soon as its leg was free, the chicken darted forward to try and bite me. I yanked my hand back, "Yeah, you're welcome I guess. You think you got out, huh? Is this the life you imagined for yourself?"

It puffed out its chest, squawked in my face, and ran away back into the bushes.

"Good luck," I muttered. I held the chain in my hand, unraveling it to reveal the full necklace with its broken clasp. The heart charm was covered in small, dirty crystals, a few missing. I chipped some of the dried mud off it with my finger and stuffed the necklace into my coat pocket.

I got back home to an empty, but silent yard. I walked up the driveway and past George's truck to find fresh, muddy footprints stamped all over my porch. I clambered up the front steps and noticed the new prints looked different than usual. They were smaller than George's grubby work boots. These prints were in two triangles, like pointy, heeled shoes. I walked around back, following the steps across my porch and saw her sitting on the swing.

Her hair was down, covered in leaves and sticks. Her green dress was dirty, and her hands were folded in her lap. Her eyes were downcast and right at her crown was a large gash. I was taken aback for a moment before I recognized the smear of pink lipstick half washed off of her gray, bloated face.

"Ginny Lewis," I called softly. She lifted her eyes to mine. They were clouded over and flickering briefly between me and the back of the house. She lifted a dirty hand up to her neck and rubbed it. There was bruising wrapped around her neck in the shape of two large hands. "I found your necklace," I said gently. "It was out in the woods, do you want it back?" She didn't move from the bench, although her whole form flickered like a candle. "Can you talk at all?"

She didn't respond. Ginny sat on the swing as it rocked in the wind, like she was pushing it herself. "I can't do anything for you," I said. "I don't know why you came all the way out here." She remained still, her cloudy, dead eyes locked with mine. The wound above her eyes was covered in dirt, blood smeared around it like she had tried to wipe it off and make herself presentable again. "You should go find that detective, sniffing around. Maybe he can do something," I shooed her off, but she didn't move. "I can't help you, Ginny."

I backed away from her and into the house. The whole time she remained, just sitting on the bench outside, staring off at nothing. Inside, the heat burned against my frozen skin. I shed off my coat and shoes, listening for any knocking or rattling, but nothing happened. I pulled back the kitchen curtain and peeked out onto the porch. She was still there, sitting and swinging. Every now and then she raised a flickering arm up to adjust her hair or rub at her face. The gash on her head was slowly oozing down her face.

I thought about calling Erik, I really did. But it was too close to where George was, and it'd be a shame to drag all that up. I took Ginny's necklace out of my pocket and left it by the sink. Maybe I could go back out later and toss it somewhere near a road or something. But for now, I stayed inside. I closed up the curtains and left Ginny alone on the swing where she was still flickering and rocking. I heated up a can of soup and got a beer out of the fridge. I left the TV off while I ate. When my eyes started to droop, I picked up my knitting needles. Elva's scarf was almost done, a thick long tube of dark blue with only a couple knots. It was actually coming along pretty nice, only a couple gaps here and there. Maybe I could try a pair of mittens next or something. The clack of my needles coming together filled the silence of the house and I waited to see if anyone would come knocking.

A Pause Before Proceeding

Perfection is a condemned building sitting at the corner of Fullerton and Greenleaf. The title is engraved into a marble plaque that rests just above the grand, wooden door which is carved with ornate patterns. There are marble columns framing the entrance as well, although they are missing sizable chunks.

The inside of Perfection has been scraped out, torn down, and redesigned more times than anyone can remember. Perfection has been a sunglasses boutique, a travel agency, a pet hotel, and briefly, an artisanal sandwich shop. Now, it sits empty. There are chains on the doors and wooden boards nailed over broken windows. Leah passes Perfection every day on her way home from work. It's her own private joke, to look at the crumbling facade and whisper 'simply perfect' to herself as she walks by.

Leah was running late today. Her train was delayed and the second she stepped off the platform it started raining. She hurried down the sidewalk in an effort to get home before her thin jacket completely soaked through. She stomped around a couple who was moving far too slowly to be taking up so much of the sidewalk, whipped around a corner, and caught her foot on something. Leah tumbled forward and landed on her hands and knees. She felt the uncomfortable press of wet pavement into her palms. She quickly righted herself and grimaced at the sting of scrapes on her hands. Leah looked down at her feet and saw what had tripped her. Another chunk of wall had fallen off Perfection's side, landing right in her path. Leah groaned and kicked it, feeling her toes crunch in her already uncomfortable boots.

Neetal already had dinner delivered by the time she got in. Leah offered a rushed hello and then locked herself in the bathroom. She peeled off her wet clothes and tossed them over the bathtub, drying off with a large, fluffy towel. She washed her hands and applied a cream to the shallow cuts on her palms. Leah squeezed as much water out of her hair as she could before combing and applying her scalp oil and deep conditioner, wrapping her hair back up in a satin hood. She ignored the small clump of hair that came loose as she combed the product through with her fingers. It's all normal, she reminded herself. Normal, normal, normal. Normal like the little lines at the corner of her mouth and the new mole on her shoulder. Normal. Normal. Normal. Leah washed her face and applied her toner, her serum, her spot treatment, her eye cream, and her night cream. Dressed in dry pajamas and with a clean face, she went back to the living room and finally kissed Neetal hello.

"Did you order from the usual?" she asked. He had pulled their food out of the takeout bag and was opening containers on the kitchen counter.

"I thought you wanted to order from Chouzhang Express this time?"

"Yeah, I was just checking that you remembered," she winked at him. Neetal rolled his eyes playfully.

"The delivery fee was almost eight dollars. Why didn't we just pick up from down the street, again?"

"I wanted the chive dumplings." Leah batted her eyes at Neetal who grumbled half-heartedly. Leah split their food between two plates and slid one over across the counter. Neetal caught her hand and turned it over, raising an eyebrow at the scratches on her palm. "I tripped walking home," she explained. He pressed a short kiss to her hand before releasing it. They took their plates to the couch and settled into comfortable silence while they ate.

"So, are you feeling ready for tomorrow?" Neetal asked eventually.

"Sure! It'll be great," Leah mumbled back, too cheerfully, around a mouthful of noodles. She offered a thumbs up with chopsticks in hand.

Neetal laughed, "Great!"

"Great," Leah smiled back again.

"Great," Neetal echoed, then caught himself, "I'm glad. Then, next weekend I have that work thing I have to talk at. Are you still okay with coming?"

"Of course. It sounds great."

Neetal chatted a bit more about work, which coworkers were competing for a promotion and who had forgotten to button their pants after using the bathroom. Leah tried to listen attentively, barely bouncing her knee or fidgeting with her fingernails. Every now and then her eyes would drift across the room back to their takeout bag waiting on the counter. When they finished eating, she hurried to clear their plates and grab the bag again. She eagerly turned it upside down and watched as five fortune cookies fell onto the coffee table. She lined them up carefully and turned to Neetal.

"You want to pick first?" she offered. He shook his head and gestured for her to go ahead, all part of the routine.

Leah wiggled her fingers between them, considering for a minute, then picked the one farthest to the right. She unwrapped the cookie and broke it neatly in half, extracting the small piece of paper.

"So, what miraculous wisdom have you received?" Neetal joked. Leah was holding her paper delicately, mouth agape.

"There's no way, absolutely no way." Leah held up the completely blank scrap of paper from inside her cookie.

"Huh, again?" Neetal laughed, "What is that? Five times in a row? Some luck you have." He must have seen something in her face because he stopped laughing almost instantly. "You know it doesn't mean anything, right? You could pick another cookie, we have, like, a lot more."

"It doesn't work like that!" Leah stood up from the couch.

"Well, they're cookies, so I think you can make it work however you want."

"We even ordered from across the city! How does this keep happening?"

"I knew you didn't only want chive dumplings," Neetal accused, "Seriously?"

"This is not normal! Why are they blank? Why only the ones I pick?" Leah paced in front of the couch as she spoke, "At the very least, admit this is bizarre."

Neetal sighed and pulled his lip between his teeth which he always did when he was calculating something. He bobbed his head side to side a couple times while Leah glared at him.

"Well, I'm guessing there's a supplier somewhere that most of the local places order from and they ran out of ink for a batch." He shrugged, "I still don't think it means anything."

"It's a bad omen is what it is," she insisted. This was getting ridiculous, they ordered takeout every Thursday, usually from Rose's, a Chinese restaurant down the street. For weeks now, blank fortunes had been piling up. It wasn't normal. She had tried ignoring it the first couple of times, but then *the dinner* happened. Now, Leah was forgetting her umbrella and breaking out on her forehead. She was stuttering on phone calls, breaking dishes in the sink, and the handle of her favorite purse had ripped. Leah groaned and plopped back onto the couch, "Mom said I should burn some bay leaves and cleanse my energy."

"Your mom rings those awful bells in my ears every time we go over to help me hear the angels." Neetal made a face.

"Does it ever work?"

"Maybe. If angels sound like tinnitus." Leah smiled a bit at that. "Look, you know those things are completely phony right?"

"Yes," she grumbled.

"Even if they weren't, a blank cookie doesn't necessarily mean something bad is going to happen. If anything, it means nothing is going to happen."

"And how is that better?"

"Well, that's like free will, isn't it? Nothing is ever guaranteed. We hardly have any control over our own lives if you think about it. No matter what you do, sometimes, the results are just random. Embrace the chaos."

"That sounds awful," Leah threw her head back against the couch. Neetal laughed again and patted Leah's knee where it sat pressed against his on the sofa.

Leah had been the one to ask out Neetal, almost six years ago, back in college. She would get up in the middle of the night to go for a walk when she was feeling restless, and he was always there in their dorm floor's lounge, watching TV or eating out of a takeout container. They spent most of the semester waving at each other as Leah waited for the elevator. He was always gone by the time she came back, until one night he was still there, slumped over on the crappy couch, asleep. Leah had knocked on the window and he had startled awake, almost falling off the couch. Leah had asked him to get a drink with her as they picked scattered fried rice out of the carpet.

Neetal was disorganized, easily flustered, and only wore four different t-shirts that were all the same color. But, he had finally learned how to shape his facial hair to suit his jawline and bought jeans in the right size. He joined a book club that met every Tuesday at his friend's house and went out with coworkers on the weekends. Leah's friends were mostly all out of state now, working at marketing firms and news agencies. She had spent the last two years stuck at a call center, trying to get interviews at law firms while Neetal got promoted to manager at the tech start-up he worked at. Leah was proud of him, she really was, but she was also tired. A kind of bone tired that settled into her chest and made it hard to breathe sometimes if she thought too hard about it. So, usually she didn't think about it.

Leah yawned and slumped against Neetal where they sat watching TV. He wrapped an arm around her shoulders and squeezed gently. She hummed and buried her face closer, into the crutch of his neck.

"Bedtime?" he teased. Leah nodded against him.

They brushed their teeth together and climbed into their respective sides of their large, king-sized bed. The big bed was a priority, despite the fact that it took up a ridiculous amount of space in their tiny bedroom. Neither of them liked to touch when they slept, and this guaranteed a healthy amount of distance. Neetal scrolled on his phone and Leah put on her weighted sleep mask. Once she got comfortable, she nudged her leg back and patted Neetal's calf with her foot. He reached over and rubbed her leg.

"You know, if you feel nervous about tomorrow at all, you can tell me," he said softly. Leah kicked him gently.

"I feel fine, really." Leah pulled her leg away and curled further onto her side, "Goodnight," she whispered.

"Goodnight," Neetal whispered back, "Sleep well. I don't want you to complain about under-eye bags in all our photos."

"Ha, ha. You know I'd just edit them out."

Neetal snorted and she heard him turn off the lamp. Leah let the quiet rumble of their fan fill her ears, joined quickly by Neetal's soft snoring. She spent a couple hours laying still, then tossing and turning, before giving up and making her way back into the kitchen. She turned on the kettle for tea and started getting together the ingredients for chocolate chip cookies.

Nighttime baking had become a bit of a habit. Whenever Leah's mind was racing too much to sleep, baking gave her something to do with her hands and a set of easy rules to follow. Leah tried not to think about how she really would have bags under her eyes in all their photos at dinner tomorrow. Their *engagement* dinner, with engagement photos and both of their parents there. It's not like they weren't already engaged, but there hadn't been a chance to take pictures the first time around.

It wasn't Neetal's fault. It was Leah's hair, which had started coming out in the shower in clumps and she wasn't sure what that meant. Vitamin deficiency? Stress? Parasites? She had meant to keep the hair just for a little while to take a picture for the doctor. Using a ziplock bag felt too serial killer-esque and if it was out in the open Neetal would have asked about it. Then, he would have explained in his *I optimize search engines* voice about how storing away clumps of hair was something only disturbed people did.

So yes, Leah hid a ring box filled with her hair in their dresser. She had the box leftover from a birthday present and it seemed like the best option. Her hair box was small, red, and startlingly similar to Neetal's engagement ring box. Unknown to each other, they were hiding them in the same drawer. For weeks, Leah snuck wads of hair into her box each night, too nervous to call the doctor for nothing and too nervous to get rid of it.

She got her first blank fortune. Then, her second. She spent more and more time in the bathroom after Neetal had gone to bed, combing through each strand and looking for bald spots. Every piece that came loose, she stuffed it into her box, hoping that somehow preserving it there would save her from losing anything else.

She knew the proposal was coming. Neetal had booked a dinner for them and their parents a month in advance at a stupidly fancy restaurant and slyly offered to pay for her to go get her nails done. Leah had spent the whole taxi ride to dinner mentally preparing her speech and practicing her earnestly surprised smile in the rearview mirror. When the restaurant's violinist came over to their table and Neetal slid out of his chair, Leah braced herself. He popped open the ring box and all of her hair had come springing out in dark knots like little spiders. It blew all over Neetal, covering his suit in a netting of dark hair. Leah's Mom had gasped and muttered something about signs from the universe while he sat there with her hair hanging off his beard, staring at her. The whole restaurant was completely silent aside from one table that had remained clapping through the whole thing. There had been one awkward brunch with his parents since and a couple video chats between Leah and her mother where neither had mentioned it.

Leah sat with her tea while her cookies baked and listened to the rain still falling outside. She stretched out on the couch and let her arm dangle off the side, almost touching the floor. The streetlights outside cast the shadow of water droplets onto her rug and she traced the small circles and streaks with her finger. When the oven timer finally beeped, she realized her other arm had fallen asleep.

The rainstorms continued all through the night and the next day. Leah trudged her way through work and now she only had half an hour to get home, change, and leave again to meet Neetal at the restaurant. She rushed down the sidewalk, rounded the corner, but stopped when she reached Perfection. She glared up at the looming building and muttered, "Simply perfect," rolling her eyes. Leah stood on the corner with the wind threatening to blow her umbrella out of her grip. She peered down the street and could see her building with its large bushes and iron gate. But instead of going home, she turned around and crossed the street the other way. She walked against the wind two blocks down to Rose's. Leah stood in front of the small restaurant and caught a flash of Mindy, the owner, and one of the chefs behind the counter. She noticed and waved. Leah walked inside.

The restaurant was empty and only half decorated, with posters of the different dishes they made and some doodles kids had done on the paper menus. The other half had booths covered in plastic sheets where a mural of cranes standing in a pond was partially completed. Mindy was behind the counter, drinking a mug of tea and folding up to-go boxes.

"Good to see you, even though it's not Thursday. Want your usual order?" Mindy asked.

"That's okay," Leah replied. She rocked on her heels, "Actually, could I just get a strawberry smoothie? And maybe a fortune cookie?"

Leah sat on one of the yellow, metal bar-stools in front of the window with her umbrella dripping onto the floor where it leaned against the wall. She sipped her smoothie and watched the incessant rainfall coming down outside. Neetal had texted her for an update ten minutes ago and she had not replied yet. Taking a deep breath, Leah took her fortune cookie and unwrapped it carefully. She cracked it open neatly in half and pulled out the slip of paper.

When all else fails, things will come to pass.
Lucky # 46, 84, 3, 11, 24, 8   Learn Chinese: Rain
Yǔ 雨

Her phone rang in her coat pocket. Neetal was probably calling from the restaurant wondering where she was. It was almost time for their reservation and she was still at least forty minutes away, if she left right now, all wet and frizzy looking. She declined the call. Leah crumpled her nonsense fortune into her damp hand.

She imagined everyone waiting for her. Leah's mother was probably in some stuffy coat with her arms crossed and her husband would be playing some loud game on his phone. Her dad and Neetal's dad would be talking about golf and Neetal's mom would be fussing over his hair that she always thought was too long.

Outside, people were running down the sidewalk, their raincoats a swirling array of color. Others moved slower, umbrellas getting blown back by the wind. Raindrops were spattering against the restaurant window, blurring the details of faces and bodies and leaving only shapes. They reminded her of the mismatched, rolly beads her mother kept in a cookie tin beside her sewing machine. Leah would sit on the floor and shake the tin, transfixed on the way all the beads would swirl together like a kaleidoscope. She would sit there, staring and shaking them around, until her mom could no longer stand the noise and would snatch the tin away.

Leah raised her hands into a cup around her eyes and stared outside. She shook her hands softly against her face and watched as all the people-shaped-blobs outside wiggled. They rolled around her vision, blurring together into a swirl of meaningless colors and shapes. Through the binocular of her hands, she caught a glimpse of her own reflection in the window and laughed. Her hair was completely ruined and her face shined with grease from the humidity. Her makeup had sweat off except a little clumpy liner left around her eyes. She wiped the makeup from under her eyes and remembered her discarded fortune paper.

She peeled the crumpled, damp fortune off the table and looked at it again. The ink had bled, mushing the words together in a watery mess, leaving the paper blank and gray. Leah squished it into a gummy blob and tossed it into her empty smoothie cup. Outside, people continued to fight against the rain to get wherever it was they were going. Leah smoothed down her hair, threw away her cup, and waved goodbye to Mindy. Wrapping her coat tighter around her waist and opening her umbrella, Leah pushed the door open and headed back into the storm.

Apophenia

When Sania registered that the train had stopped again, it was much darker than before. She shot up in her seat and looked out the window, only to find her own surprised expression reflected back at her against the now dark sky. Sania rushed to grab her bag and jumped off just as the doors shut behind her. The train pulled away, leaving her alone on the platform.

It was completely empty, lit up by overhead lights, and raised up above a sea of dark, sweeping cornfields. Off on the horizon she could make out the distinct glow of a highway backlit by the final rays of sunset. Sania set her bag down on the platform, heavy with the cookies she had bought earlier for her sister and other trinkets. She adjusted her headscarf which had come loose during her nap and rubbed her eyes, wincing when her hands came away with eyeliner smeared on them.

Sania did not completely recognize the area; she knew there were farm fields out this way, but had only ever driven past them. Some of her friends used to go to parties out in the back fields, taking little foot paths through the rows of corn and soybeans. She supposed it could be worse. Sania could see ahead, a wide path through one of the cornfields that looked like it went all the way to the highway.

She hesitated at the thought of walking more, especially with all her stuff, but waiting for another train this late sounded worse. Resolutely, she hiked her bag further up on her shoulder, walked down the stairs and left the station. There wasn't much around, just a cafe with a flickering closed sign and a dark, locked-up ticket booth. As she reached the station's edge, pavement bled into patchy grass and gravel. Sania paused at the edge of the cornfield and peered down the path as far as she could. She was sure she could make out the highway lights straight ahead. It would be a quick walk.

She stayed in between two neat rows of corn, keeping to the dirt road. It was narrower than she had thought from up high, only just enough space for her and her bag. Ripening husks loomed overhead, the occasional stalk curving down over the path forcing her to duck under it. Sania kept her arms tucked in front of her and her eyes fixed down on the path. The fields were denser up close than they had looked from the platform. Sania's feet were starting to get tired again. Looking back, she could no longer see the lights from the train station nor could she see any highway lights ahead of her.

It was dark in the unlit field and it had gotten colder. Fog rolled in around her, obscuring Sania's view to almost nothing. She waded through thick, cloudy blackness that left her squinting and stumbling over loose gravel. She tried to shine her phone's flashlight onto the path, but it couldn't penetrate the fog. It felt like she had been out here for a while. The main road had to be close by. Surely it was coming up soon and there would be streetlights, cars, and a bus station. She kept waiting to see the lights.

A sudden rustling sound off in the corn startled her. Sania stopped walking for a moment, straining her ears, but it was already gone. The dark was playing tricks on her somehow, making her feel like there were creatures lurking about. The rustling sounded again, closer this time. She held her breath. It was nothing. Another, this time a crunching snap of leaves. It was just a bird, or maybe a field mouse. Sania stepped forward and heard someone else step onto the path behind her.

"Hello?" she whirled around, "I can't see anything." Sania reached out in front of her and brushed against the rough leaves of another corn stalk. She jerked her hand back.

"You shouldn't say you can't see anything, even if it's true. At least pretend you are more aware." The voice came from behind her. Sania tried to turn herself towards it, unsure now what direction she was even facing in the fog.

"Listen, I will kick you so hard, man! Leave me alone," she growled.

"You can't kick me if you can't see me," the voice chided. "Here, I'll make this a little easier." The blinding fog pulled back, leaving a clear circle of a couple yards around her. Sania blinked rapidly, clearing the wet film from her eyes. She was alone in the circle until a small creature moved inside. It had a narrow snout, whiskers, and one beady, black eye while the other socket was empty and scarred over. It crawled its furry body towards her and Sania took one huge step back.

"Gross, rabies," she muttered. The creature sat on its hind legs and pressed one white paw to its chest.

It scoffed, "I do not have rabies, but even if I did that would be the least of your problems right now."

Sania gaped at it, "You're the one talking to me?"

"Yes."

"You're a rat!"

The creature rolled its one eye, flicked its long, skinny tail and bared its teeth, "I am an opossum."

"Why are you talking?" She looked around her clear circle, the fog surrounding her like a solid wall. "How are you keeping the fog away?" Sania thought back to the crafts fair she which had come from downtown. The chance that she had eaten anything drugged was slim, but not impossible. Sania squeezed her eyes shut and took a deep breath, but when she opened them again nothing about the scene had changed. The creature sighed deeply and slowly at her like it was exhausted.

"My hold on the fog won't last forever, so we should keep moving." The rat-thing, *opossum,* started to walk, and the clearing followed it. Rather than be lost in the dark again Sania kept up, walking closely behind.

"Do you actually know your way out of here?" she asked. It did not bother to turn back, sniffing the ground as it led them ahead.

"Of course I do. But I need something from you to do it," it said.

"What?"

"May I have your name?"

"Sania. And you are?" It felt impolite not to ask for a name back.

"You may call me Pos."

"Pos, like *opossum*?" she couldn't help but laugh.

He flicked his tail. "No," Pos replied shortly.

"Are you like, a wizard or something?" Pos didn't respond. Sania glared at the back of his head, "I was just checking." They walked on, Pos leading them down a dirt road between corn stalks that was always perfectly wide enough for them both, though Sania was sure it was not going in a straight line. Her legs were tired and she had no idea how long she'd been outside wandering through the corn. "Are we almost there?" Sania asked. Pos's whiskers twitched. He raised a paw and signaled her to stop walking again. "What now?"

"Hold on a moment, be very quiet," Pos whispered. Sania held her breath and listened. There were shuffling steps just outside their little bubble of clarity. The sound of crunching footsteps and a low growl circled around them. Then it was quiet again. "Very good, Sania."

"What was that?"

"We don't have much time left. I told you I needed something from you."

"Okay?"

"I need my eye to get us out of here." He raised a paw to his empty socket, scratching at it with sharp claws. Sania stared at him blankly. "I need my eye back," Pos repeated.

"Yeah, I heard you?"

"You have my eye." Sania stopped walking abruptly. Pos continued and she was almost pushed back into the fog. Sania stomped forward again,

"Excuse me? I don't have anyone's eye. That's disgusting," she replied, indignant. Pos only sighed again,

"Sania, you're familiar with this area, correct?"

"Yes, what does that matter?"

"Do you know where you are right now?" he asked.

"Yes," she shouted, exasperated. "I'm in the fields just outside of town. There's a highway nearby with a bus station. I could see it from the train platform."

"Nearby, but we haven't come to it yet?" he pressed.

"It must be a bit further than I thought..."

"I'm afraid we won't be getting anywhere if that thing out there has anything to say about it. It has been hunting me for a very long time. I can get away by changing my form, but I need my eye to do so. Then, once I've changed, I can lead us both out of here."

"And you think I have your eye?"

Pos came closer to Sania and sniffed the air, reaching up and sniffing her bag,

"Take the bracelet you bought earlier out of your bag, Sania." She didn't bother to ask how he knew she had gotten a bracelet at the market. Sania tossed her bag on the ground, rubbing the ache out of her shoulder from carrying it for so long. Reaching around the bottom, she pulled out the bracelet. It was a delicate golden band with small black and blue beads on it. The center bead was larger, a pearly color that shimmered even in the dark.

"This is your eye?" she held it up skeptically.

"Give it to me."

Sania clutched the bracelet tightly, "And then you'll be able to take me to a bus station?" Pos nodded and stuck out one of his paws.

"Fine, take it," she huffed. She bent down and handed the bracelet to Pos. He took it in his two front paws, sitting on his hind legs to sniff at it. He picked the bracelet up, dangled it above his open mouth for a moment, and then swallowed it whole. A shiver went down his spine and Pos began to cough, foaming at the mouth. For a long minute his whole body shook violently until he wretched his head backwards and Sania heard the snapping of bone.

She watched, frozen, as Pos fell over into a creaking, trembling mass of flesh and fur. Finally, he went limp. His body sagged into the dirt and his one eye rolled back into his skull. Sania reached out to touch him when out of his slack mouth, a moth flew. It was gray with mottled brown spots all over and a pearly sheen. The moth hovered above Pos's body, fluttering its tiny wings.

"Pos?" she asked. The moth flew up and circled around her once. Then, it took off.

Instantly, the circle of clarity was gone and Sania was swallowed again by fog. She stood up from where she had crouched over Pos's body, stumbling back over her bag and landing in the dirt. She shouted out his name to no answer. "I can't see you anymore!" There was nothing in the opaque darkness except the sound of her own ragged breathing. Even the crickets had stopped chirping. She picked herself up and brushed the dirt from her hands. Cautiously, Sania stepped forward and heard again the crunching of footsteps from out in the corn.

Sania grabbed her bag, reaching out to feel the edge of the path to guide her along. The footsteps continued, the sound of them seeming to surround her, spiraling in closer and then farther. It was impossible to tell which direction they were coming from. She heard a deep, low growl that echoed out through the field.

"Pos?" Sania whispered into the darkness. Sill, nothing answered her. She felt the hairs stand up on the back of her neck. Pushing her arms out, she turned, running into the corn, something sharp grazing her ankle.

Sania ran through the corn as fast as she could. Jagged husks scratched her face and snagged on her headscarf. She twisted through the field without direction. Behind her, the growling continued growing closer and closer. Finally, she spotted where the fog was thinning out. Sania's hands hit the open air and she pushed through the last of the vapor, tumbling out at the cornfield's edge.

There was a wide, empty highway in front of her, lit up by one dim, flickering streetlight. Barely looking, Sania ran across the street and collapsed into the dirt on the other side. Her lungs were burning and her eyes were stinging from all the dust. Sania rubbed down her face with her sleeve and tried to fix her headscarf as best she could. Back across the road, the field she had been in still had a cloud of fog hanging over it. The fields next to it remained clear. Behind them, Sania could clearly see the train station platform where she had started from. She stared at it, wondering how she could have gotten so lost for so long.

Through the fog, a large fox emerged. It stood halfway out of the corn, peering across the road. It had deep russet fur and sharp teeth that gleamed in the dim light. Its eyes landed on Sania and it growled deep in its throat.

As it raised up on its haunches, ready to leap forward, a large truck sped down the highway, rushing between Sania and the fox. When it was gone, so was the fox. Sania looked around wildly, trying to see where it had gone, but there was no sign of it anymore. Sania waited a moment to catch her breath before standing up and trying to brush the dirt from her clothing. She picked up her bag and started to walk in the same direction as the truck, away from the flickering streetlight and towards the soft glow of town shining on the horizon.

...

Charlie never stopped on his overnight loads. He operated on the strict philosophy that the quicker he got where he was going, the quicker he could go to sleep. But, he had skipped lunch today to get a haircut and needed to eat something soon before he keeled over going sixty miles an hour, so he begrudgingly pulled into the next diner he saw with a big enough lot to park his truck.

Hanging over the diner was a giant wooden sign of a pig's head with an apple in its mouth. It had once been nicely painted, but wind and rain had worn away the color. It had two lightbulbs for eyes with one out, leaving the pig with one glowing eye. There were pink neon letters spelling out LOTTIE'S underneath.

Charlie walked into the fluorescent dining area and chose a booth in the back over the too-small-and-squeaky looking red pleather stools at the bar. He blinked against the brightness, eyes adjusting to the stark white, gleaming floors and equally white walls littered with vintage signs and pictures. He had barely settled into the booth when a short, stocky woman with dirty-blonde, curly hair came rushing over.

"Hey Sweetie, would you like any coffee?" she drawled with a sharp, nasal voice.

"Thank you, please." He moved his coffee cup closer for her to fill. The woman bent over, pouring the coffee. Charlie kept his eyes fixed to the name tag that read 'Shirley' pinned right on top of her cleavage. He swallowed and looked away quickly as she rose back up.

"Thank you, ma'am."

"Oh, none of that, sugar. Just Shirley is fine." She pointed down at her name tag, "What else can I get started for you?"

"Three eggs over easy, some toast, dark, and sausage patties if you've got them, please."

"Sure thing, honey." Shirley winked and disappeared into the kitchen. Charlie pulled his eyes away from where he was watching her legs to drink his coffee. It was burning hot and sort of watery tasting.

Looking out the diner window, Charlie couldn't see much outside. It was like he was in a fishbowl with a fat, old, scruffy man in need of a shave looking back at him. There was a cream soda ad hanging above his head where a skinny, red-haired girl was standing in a bikini, drinking soda, on a surfboard.

"Foggy night, isn't it?" Shirley spoke from behind him. Charlie startled and turned. She had reappeared at the end of his table with the coffee pot to refill the coffee he had barely touched.

"I guess so," he replied. Visibility was awful now that he looked closer. A distant cloud hung low over the farming fields across from the diner. It hadn't been there when he parked, he was sure.

"Never liked it much, foggy nights. Too spooky for me," Shirley waved her hands in front of her, still holding the coffee pot. "My mother used to tell stories about nights like this, all sorts of weird things happen, she'd say, and she lived out in the fields before this highway even existed, so I believe her. No sir, best not to mess with it. Have to keep your wits about you, that's what I always say."

Charlie nodded, unsure how to respond. Seemingly satisfied, Shirley turned around and disappeared back into the kitchen. When Charlie turned back to look out the window, some of the fog had dissipated, leaving silhouettes of corn stalks swaying in the night breeze.

Terrible coffee aside, the food was actually very good. Charlie promptly ordered a piece of cherry pie, after the eggs, at Shirley's recommendation. He kept drinking the coffee too. Every time he got halfway through a cup, Shirley would come back out with the pot. She had been making small talk, lingering at the end of his booth. He thought it might be nice to get her number, maybe offer to buy her a drink when he was coming back through town. Charlie took a long swig and sure enough, she emerged, coffee pot in hand.

"Hey doll, this'll be my last cup. I've got to hit the road soon," he told her.

"Alright then, I'll go ahead and bring the check over. Where are you headed?"

"Mankato, I come through here pretty often. You from around here?"

"Yessir, born and raised. I left for a few years when I got married. I'm divorced now and back home. I take care of my mother."

"Do you know any good bars around?" Charlie asked, but Shirley was still talking,

"Mama had a stroke last year and now she can't even dress or use the bathroom on her own. I've got a brother, but he's out West, so I'm stuck with her. You know how it is." Charlie sucked his lip between his teeth.

"That's nice, honey. You got a number? Maybe I can ring you up when I'm driving back through, take you out for a drink?" Shirley carried on like she hadn't even heard him.

"Last night I was over with Mama, I made her cornbread casserole for dinner, but she kept drooling it all back out. I haven't seen anything like that in my life. I don't have the money for a nurse, I'm all she's got. I'm seeing her again tomorrow. I've got to try and brush her hair out before she gets all matted up. They warn you about that stuff you know, if you stay in bed too long your hair falls out and you get sores in unsavory areas."

"Right," Charlie mumbled.

"It really makes you think, is that what's waiting at the end of the road for us all? Just a spit-soaked pillow and someone else putting your bloomers on for you? Anyways, I'll bring that check over for you, sugar." She patted his shoulder and walked off.

Charlie paid and left a nice enough tip on the table. Back outside, he leaned up against the wall of the diner and lit up a cigarette. Charlie looked out at the empty highway while he smoked, watching the occasional car or truck pass by. No one else ever pulled into Lottie's. He smoked and enjoyed the quiet night, until a low thumping prompted him to look up. A moth was butting up against one of the diner windows. Over, and over again, it flew right up against the window, trying to get at the bright light inside. It kept going, like each try could be the one where it finally broke through the glass. Charlie watched, transfixed, until it finally gave up and flew away.

Charlie walked out to his truck after stamping his cigarette butt. He fished around for his keys, realizing he couldn't feel his wallet. He turned out all his pockets but still couldn't find it.

As he looked around the ground by his feet and behind him, all the lights in the diner shut off at once. He was left alone in the dark, lit only by the LOTTIE'S sign and its pig with one eye. Cursing under his breath, Charlie stomped over to the diner's window, but he couldn't see inside. He pulled on the door and found it locked. Charlie walked around the whole building, coming back to the front to pound on the door, when he noticed his wallet on the ground. There was nothing left in it but his driver's license. Charlie cursed again, loudly this time, and departed with one last bang on the door, staring out at his truck, still sitting alone in the vacant lot. That's what he got for making a stop on an overnight run.

Standing at the edge of the parking lot, he kicked at the dirt and listened for any cars. He had no idea where that waitress could have gone without him seeing her or a car. He was fuming mad and planted himself down beneath the LOTTIE'S sign, waiting for anyone to exit the dark diner. The neon sign was buzzing loudly above him, and the road was quiet except for the sounds of distant traffic. Charlie rolled his eyes, kicking at the ground again. Screw it, he thought. There was no use in standing out here all night. He spit into the dirt and was about to return to the truck when a shuffling sound from down the road stopped him.

A young woman was walking off to the side of the road. She looked a little worse for wear, her clothes were disheveled, and she limped slightly. She had her hair and shoulders covered with a dark orange scarf. As she got closer, he saw leaves hanging off of it and a tear at the bottom. She turned behind her periodically, like she was looking to see if she was being followed. Charlie cleared his throat and the girl jumped.

"Hey Miss," Charlie shouted out to her. "You need some help?" The girl stopped walking, turning to stare at him with wide eyes. She looked him over, saying nothing. "Are you okay?" he called again. "What's your name?" The girl stared at him another minute then gently shook her head.

"Do you know how far it is back into town?" the girl asked.

"I think it's a couple miles north? There should be a bus station or something that way." Charlie pointed down the road. "Do you need a lift?" The girl shook her head again.

She continued down the street, walking past him without looking back anymore. Charlie watched until he couldn't see her. Her orange headscarf fading away slowly, until it was just a single dot of color against the steely gray sky and black pavement. Charlie got back in his truck and started to drive. He drove East. Around him, fog swirled low along the road and covered the surrounding farm fields. The horizon turned a hazy red as the sun slowly rose out of the fog in front of him, like an eye, blinking itself awake.

Small Talk

Cindy smoothed her skirt down for the tenth time, pressing her palms over her kneecaps, and digging her fingernails into the flesh there.

"Thanks again for driving me home," she said with a small smile. Tom kept his eyes on the road and shrugged slightly.

"It's really no trouble, I'm headed back this way too."

"That's right, you mentioned you live near the library?"

"Yeah," he replied with another shrug. The car was as quiet as the restaurant had been, but at least then they'd had the chatter of other people around. Now, there was only the sound of Tom's squeaky brakes and the wind pushing insistently past the car. When they first got in, the radio had been turned so loud Cindy had jumped and Tom had sheepishly shut it off entirely. Now, she almost wished for the music back.

"The restaurant was pretty good," she offered. "Had you been before?"

"Yeah, yeah it was. Never been, mostly I stick to AJ's when I eat out. It was good though, different. I still don't really understand why the soup was cold?"

"I think it was supposed to be? It's a gazpacho." Tom shrugged again. Cindy pressed her fingers harder into her knees.

Heather had set them up. She worked with Cindy at the youth center and knew Tom from college. He was a 'great guy' and 'really interesting, just like you', but they didn't watch the same shows or read the same books. Cindy knew nothing about fishing, and when she mentioned her crocheting Tom's face had gone entirely blank. "Do you have any other plans this week?" Cindy tried again.

"I'm going out with a few guys from work, we're going to set up some crab traps."

"That sounds nice."

"Yeah. Did you, I mean were you asking because you wanted to—you know, or were you hoping—"

"No," Cindy cut him off loudly and abruptly, backtracking, "I mean, not no to wanting to—umm, well not that I don't want to see you again, but—" she trailed off.

"Yeah, me too," Tom said quietly. "Don't worry about it," he quirked his lip into a friendly half-smile, still staring at the road. Cindy chewed on her lip. "Really, it's okay," Tom chuckled. "No hard feelings."

"Okay, thanks," Cindy laughed with him. She let her hands relax in her lap, still smoothing down the fabric repetitively.

Outside the car it was starless and dark. The road curved through the woods in two narrow lanes sided by tall, thick trees, the occasional slow zone marked for campsites. Tom drove fast, but cautiously, allowing Cindy to relax until he turned around a bend and she caught something out of the corner of her eye, standing at the tree-line. The car lights had hit it, just for a moment, and then it was behind them as Tom whizzed along the curved road.

"What was that?" she gasped.

"What?"

"You didn't see it? There was something in the woods back there. It was standing up, huge, like a bear!" The thing had been tall for sure, with a thick fur, or maybe skin, rough and dark like tree bark.

"Maybe it was a really big deer," Tom offered. "It's a little too early for bears, but I guess not impossible." He shrugged again as they sped through the woods, unfazed by whatever Cindy thought she saw.

"It didn't look *quite* like a bear."

"What? Are you telling me you saw Bigfoot?"

"Ha, ha," Cindy rolled her eyes, "there was something actually there, I saw it."

"Probably just the trees. Sometimes the car lights bounce off the woods here and it creates all kinds of wonky shadows. I can't tell you how many times I've been headed home and thought I saw something."

"And you never stop to get a closer look?" Tom's eyes never left the road, but his mouth turned back up. Cindy scrunched her fists in her lap.

"Yeah," Tom said, drawing out the word as he laughed. "I stop all the time, just like they do in those movies where people get brutally murdered."

"I told you I don't watch horror movies," Cindy replied curtly.

Tom laughed again, "Maybe you should start. They're filled with valuable life lessons."

Cindy kept her arms folded across her chest and eyes trained out the window. Eventually, they turned out of the woods and onto Cindy's street. Tom pulled into the parking lot of her apartment building and shut off the car. He turned to look at her fully and raised an eyebrow at the expression he found on her face.

"I don't mean to tease," he said.

"Yes, you do," Cindy huffed. Tom shrugged again. They said a short and polite goodnight. Cindy disappeared into her building and Tom began the familiar drive home, alone.

...

Celia had figured the day couldn't get any worse, but as usual she was mistaken. A whole week straight of no sleep at all, her insomnia worse than ever, and this was *after* the sleep specialist had given her the new pills. Now, she would have to go back to the place that charged $200 a session and asked her what *she* thought the root cause of her sleeping problems were.

To make things worse, her mother was the one who drove her here to get groceries since Celia wasn't allowed to drive until she figured out the whole medication thing. Her Mom had been all too happy to do it, *anything for my baby*, but Celia was thirty-five and too old to be driven around for errands.

Her mom had texted that she was back in the parking lot waiting for her after a run to the fabric store, but Celia had been stuck in the longest checkout line she had ever seen. There was only one lane open and the cashier working it just. Wouldn't. Stop. Talking.

She seemed to be on a personal mission to drag the life story out of every single person in line. If Celia wasn't next, she would have considered abandoning the task entirely. Finally, the man in front of her managed to escape the cashier's monolog, grabbed his hostage bags, and bid her a quick, clipped goodbye. He sped out of the store and Celia placed her basket on the conveyor belt, bracing herself.

"Good morning Miss, pleased to see you on this lovely day," the woman chirped. She looked about her Mom's age, with bright orange dyed-hair and blue eyeshadow smeared on her wrinkly eyelids almost all the way up to her eyebrows. Celia just nodded hello back and pulled out her reusable bags. She would not give in to the chatter. "Oh, somebody came prepared." the woman continued when Celia didn't respond. "That's the kind of thing we love to see. Now, Redwoods High, huh? Are you a student?" Celia looked down at the bag from her old high school.

"I was," she replied before she could stop herself. *A long time ago.* Saying anything was a mistake. The woman's eyes lit up and she clapped her hands which still hadn't even scanned a single item. Damn.

"How wonderful, my brother teaches math over there, has for about seven years now. He does the kind with all the shapes, you know, that kind of stuff. Oh, what is that called? I'm always forgetting the names of things. Oh well, I was never a math person myself." She finally picked the first items out of Celia's basket to scan as she continued to talk. "Anyways, he went out hunting a couple weeks ago with his wife's brother and his son, but they went inland instead of north. I thought that was weird. You always go north for better hunting, that's what everyone says." She stopped to slowly type in the code for Celia's bag of plums and Celia fought against the urge to close her eyes and scream.

"There it is, I always get tripped up on produce. There are so many numbers to remember. Not a math person. Anyways, they went inland, I don't know why, but they were out just doing the small critters, racoons and stuff. They sent the dogs out and were walking behind when my brother's wife's brother's son noticed something strange down in the dirt."

Celia had never wished more fervently that she could fall asleep at will. She would drop dead on the floor right here if it was an option. The cashier was placing languidly scanned groceries into her bag and Celia stood there tapping her foot, just to do something with all the restless energy she was building up. She took a deep breath and let it out slowly through her nose as the cashier continued her tale. "The boy's about eleven, so when he stopped my brother they thought he was just playing a game, but sure enough there were these unusual tracks leading further into the woods. It's way too early in the season for bears and there was no way it was a cougar or anything else. My brother said the tracks were huge, he was absolutely floored." Finally, the cashier was on the eggs, Celia's last item. She picked them up and hovered them over the scanner when the man in line behind her asked,

"Did they figure out what the tracks were?" The cashier set her eggs back down.

"No, they never did! They looked around to see where the tracks led but couldn't find anything. Must be one big critter out there somewhere, I guess. You really never know what all is living up in those woods." The woman finally, *finally* scanned the eggs and set them next to the other full bags. Celia paid and ran out to the parking lot as fast as she could without turning to say goodbye.

...

Tom was taking the bus to work today. His car was in the shop to get the brakes changed which meant he couldn't stop at his usual coffee place on the way in.

148

He'd have to go to that new place next to the office, and they always burnt their coffee. At least he had thought ahead and brought a book for the commute. As he read, Tom registered someone sitting down in the seats behind him. He tilted his head up and saw a beautiful woman with red, curly hair and a tall man with a well-groomed mustache and glasses. Tom wondered if they were together. The man wasn't bad looking per se, but his hair had too much product in it. Maybe if he got off first he could go sit by the woman and introduce himself.

"How was the party Friday night?" the man asked.

The woman brushed a stray curl behind her ear, "It didn't happen," she replied. Her voice was nice, deep but not gruff. Tom kept his eyes fixed on his book but wasn't paying much attention to the words on the page.

"What do you mean?" the man asked her.

"I mean, I went, but I never found it. I got ready, drove all the way out, and when I got there it was just an empty field. I knew it was an underground kind of thing, but I was expecting, like, a sign at least or something."

"Weird, were there other people around?" the man asked. Tom was thankful he was keeping her talking, since he liked her voice. Maybe they were just friends after all? Or work colleagues.

"That's the thing, there were cars parked and stuff. At first, I thought maybe I had gone to the wrong place, but then I saw some lights coming through the woods."

"Do not tell me you walked into the woods to find a mysterious party. That is how people get stabbed, Katie."

"That is also why I carry a switchblade, Steven," the woman, Katie, replied pointedly. Tom bit his lip to keep from snorting. He could appreciate a woman who held her own. He turned his head a little to look toward the window but focused his gaze on the people behind him. The guy didn't have his arm around her or anything. Katie licked her bottom lip and continued, "Anyways, I did walk through the woods, I figured there was a cabin or something where the party was and maybe I'd missed it on the flyer or whatever."

"So, was there?"

"I kept walking and I could see the lights, like strobe lights, and I heard music, even some people laughing, but I never actually reached them." Tom had turned back to his book and had been staring down at the same page all the while Katie told her story. He was starting to feel motion sick from the small-print words jostling along with the bus.

"What do you mean?" the man asked.

"I mean, I kept walking and walking and walking and even though I could basically feel the music, I never got there. I'm not even sure where I was, but the lights never got any closer, and when I called out to the people, no one answered me. Eventually I gave up and decided to head back. I turned around and it was like I had never left the parking lot. I walked for probably forty minutes, straight into the woods, but as soon as I turned around I was just at the edge by the field and the parking lot."

Tom closed his book and put it into his bag. He pulled the rope for the next stop, silently hoping maybe the red-haired woman would be getting off too.

"Were you high?" the man laughed.

"Shut up, I was not," Katie replied, laughing too. "It was super-freaking-weird. Get this, there weren't even any footprints in the dirt. All those cars, all the people, so why were there no footprints?"

"It sounds like you had a bad trip," the man said laughing.

"Shut up, I told you I wasn't on anything. You are so not allowed to make fun of me," Katie laughed and shoved his shoulder. "I totally thought I was going to get murdered." The bus came to a stop and Tom got up, stuffing his book into his bag. He cast one last look back at the two of them talking and laughing together before getting off the bus. It drove off while Tom waited for the light to change so he could go get his coffee.

...

Kevin was out on his regular hike. He was glad to have remembered his waterproof jacket this time as wet ferns and coffeeberry plants dragged across his arms. His legs were going to be soaked, but he knew it would feel nice as it started to warm up later. The morning fog hadn't yet faded and Kevin wiped some condensation off his forehead. This time of year it was nice and quiet out here, no tourists littering on the trails or loud families with their giant, flashy campers. He was hoping to head up-river and find some otters to get pictures of for the community center bulletin board. He hadn't been out all week, too busy with work and gearing up for the high season.

As Kevin made his way along the familiar trail he heard some rustling coming up ahead. He turned and noticed a fork that he didn't remember being there before. To the left was his usual path, heading straight, alongside the river and up the mountain, but to the right was another path that headed east, deeper into the woods. He was sure there were no trails that headed east until you got further up the mountain. More rustling came from the new path and Kevin decided to follow it.

He came out here pretty often, living in a small house just at the base of the mountain, and found it hard to believe they had managed to get a whole new trail in without him noticing. It was too wide to be made by deer, with smooth, well-packed dirt. Kevin bet that if he dug a little, he could find the same safety netting they used at the State Park. There was another bout of rustling and clanking from down the trail and Kevin knew the sounds immediately.

Campers. He recognized the sounds of a tent being disassembled and a family talking amongst themselves. He could hear children laughing and a bucket of water being poured out. Kevin may as well go say hello. It wasn't usual to get campers this early in spring, and he wanted to make sure they knew it was too soon to get in the river. Most people came out over the summer for tubing or kayaking, but right now the water was too cold with a heavy current and dangerous undertows, especially for children. It couldn't hurt to say something, even if they already knew. Just last summer a girl had drowned in the waters a few miles up. They put signs up all over the place warning people not to swim, but every year accidents happened.

Kevin kept on the path, he was surprised how level it was, not many roots or rocks to step over. The wildflowers that grew along the river had faded into large, dense ferns and thick tree trunks. Wax Myrtle spread across the ground with patches of Ithuriel's Spear despite the dense tree cover. The small pops of blue flowers peered out over the rest of the shrubs, reminding Kevin of watchful eyes. It was colder and darker over here than even the base of the mountain had been when Kevin began his hike. He glanced up, trying to glimpse the sun through the trees, but all he saw were tangled branches, weaved like a tunnel, leading him further in. He could have sworn it was supposed to be sunny today.

The family should be set up somewhere close. He could still hear them, laughing and talking and shuffling, but they didn't sound any closer than they had at the trail's start. Were they hiking too? It really sounded like people packing up, not moving down a trail. Kevin stopped walking and looked around. Something seemed off about the plants around him. Leaves swayed in the slight breeze a little too evenly, as if all the foliage was breathing and moving together in perfect time. The dirt below Kevin's feet was too smooth, the trees growing too-perfectly straight. Why was it so cold here?

The family continued to make noise, but they never seemed to move farther or closer to where he was, despite Kevin having walked about a half mile already. Kevin looked beside the trail at a large spider web stretched between a bush and a tree, pristinely decorated with dew drops but no spider. Peering further along, it only seemed to get darker. Well, it was probably okay. If that family was moving inland then there was no risk of them trying to swim. They'd be fine. Kevin was free to go back to the river and find his otters. He took in one last look at the unsettling trail and turned around.

...

Tom sat at his desk, swiveling back and forth in his chair, trying to stretch out his legs without standing up. Today had been pretty slow, but he was still biding time, trying to clock in a couple extra hours before he left to get his car. His empty coffee cup sat precariously on the edge of his desk as he scrolled on the computer. Tom had heard a couple of the finance girls talking about a concert they were going to next week in the park and he was trying to score tickets. He hoped to get two and try to bring a date. He found the link to the community events calendar and clicked it.

The first thing to pop up wasn't a calendar, but a Missing Persons notice. A guy had gone out hiking near the river last week and had never returned home. The family stated he was an experienced hiker and unlikely to become lost or injured without notifying somebody. There was an expired link to sign up for a search party but no other updates since.

Geez, there was always something going on. It seemed like every month there was some new disappearance or dead hiker story. It's part of why Tom had always preferred fishing, no chance of falling off a cliff or getting dragged off by mountain lions. Poor guy. Tom scrolled past the notice to the calendar with concerts and shows listed, pushing the missing hiker to the back of his mind as he pulled up the site to order tickets.

It was dark by the time Tom got his car back from the mechanic. Jerry had been nice as always, but the man sure could talk your ear off when he got going, and his wife was even worse. He had managed to escape without agreeing to another cup of coffee, so he still had time to stop at AJ's and grab something to eat. Tom turned into the familiar lot, it's flickering lights highlighting parking spaces littered with potholes and torn up concrete. Last fall, a rockslide had damaged the lot and they still hadn't gotten around to completely clearing all the rubble away.

Dorris's car was still parked out front, but the lights inside were off and the front door locked tight. Tom stood outside for a minute knocking, but no one was responding. It was strange for Dorris to leave her car here, even stranger for AJ's to be shut down an hour early. He hoped nothing serious had happened. Tom was heading to his car, ready to admit defeat, when he heard something coming from behind the store.

"Hello?" he called into the darkness. Tom squinted, but he couldn't make out more than the shadows of dumpsters melting into shadows of the trees above. It was a steep climb around the diner and there weren't really any trails that came by here. Most likely, just some raccoons digging around in the trash. Tom stomped over ready to scare them off, and he almost stepped on something that barely caught his eye.

Dorris's phone was laying on the ground, flipped open, and out of battery. Now that was strange. Could be she had to run off somewhere and dropped it without realizing. Tom picked it up. Least he could do was keep it safe overnight then run it back to her in the morning on the way to work. He slipped the phone into his pants pocket and turned away from the dumpsters. Last time he talked to Dorris, everything had been going fine. He knew her sister had been having some health issues but assumed that had all been cleared up. Tom would definitely have to come by early tomorrow and make sure everything was okay.

Damn raccoons had certainly had their fill. The dumpster lid was tossed open with a spilt bag of trash littered around the base. Half-eaten garbage trailed back to the tree-line and disappeared. Tom bent over, trying to scoop up the worst of it. Last thing Dorris needed was rats or some other vermin getting inside. As he was cleaning around the dumpster, Tom found a footstep in the dirt underneath an old styrofoam container. It was punched deep into the ground and wider than his own foot, longer too. It must be some animal track then, probably some poor creature laying on the edge of a highway by now. Tom didn't know much about hunting, but he had figured nothing came this far down the mountain. He finished clearing as much trash as he could and closed the dumpster for Dorris.

Back in his car, Tom drove with his eyes fixed on the road ahead. The streetlights faded behind him and he ramped up his brights to get through the stretch of dense woods. His high beams bounced off trees shrouded in darkness, reflecting the light back. Tom yawned and drummed his fingers on the wheel to the beat of the radio. He pointedly ignored how his headlights seemed to stare back and blink.

You Shouldn't Worry About the Frogs

Something needed to be done about all of the croaking. It was the middle of the night, those few precious hours between work and class where I could settle in long enough to think or maybe even sleep. At least, I would try if it wasn't for the frogs.

They should have been hibernating or dead and eaten already, it was too late in the season for frogs. When I first moved in, it was early summer and they had just been tadpoles, sitting in the murky still water of our courtyard's fountain. I figured they would get picked off by a bird or something. But, a few survived and now they never leave the fountain. They sit there with their constant croaking, just loud enough to break through any train of thought or distract from any activity I might try.

I stared up at my ceiling from where I laid on my mattress and ran a hand down my face. This was just another painful reminder that I could have lived in a dorm, around other people and already-built furniture. Instead, here I was, in the only part of the city I could afford, with a shoebox studio to call my very own. My mattress was still on the floor, the bed frame in a box somewhere around here. My books were stacked up on one wall next to another box that contained my desk, and my clothes would still be packed in my duffel bag, if I hadn't worn them and left them strewn around the floor.

The apartment was on the ground floor in a brick building covered in peeling yellow paint with a courtyard view that never shut up. A particularly loud croak cut through the brief silence and I groaned back loudly. Enough was enough. I got out of bed and picked up an empty takeout box from last night. I grabbed my keys and headed outside.

It was cold out and I was barefoot, wearing the pajamas Mom got me for Christmas last year, the ones with the bunnies all over them. Luckily, no one was around to see. I marched over to the fountain that sat at the courtyard's center, surrounded by neglected plants. It was made of crumbling cement with moss overtaking most of what was left. Old rainwater was collected in the base where the frogs sat. All five of them stopped croaking as I approached. They didn't scatter or even move, just sat there staring at me.

"Alright, listen up," I said. "One night. Tomorrow, I'm going to find a spot for you. A nice park or something and then you will stay there, and I will get some sleep. Understand?" I glared down at the frogs. One croaked, the others joined back in. It sounded enough like an agreement. I got down and scooped them up and into my takeout container, they went in without a fight.

Before I could close the lid, the iron gate creaked behind me, and I whipped around to see the door swinging open. I scrambled up from where I kneeled in the dirt and ran back inside with the frogs cradled in my arms. Shutting the front door to my section of the building, I peeked through the window. One frog jumped and I caught it with my hand, pushed it back into the container. "Quiet," I whispered to the frog. "One second." I peered from behind the curtains at the figure coming through the courtyard.

I could never quite figure out Maggie's work schedule. She was always coming and going with a backpack on one shoulder and a canvas bag on the other. She was some sort of waitress judging by the uniform, but I didn't know where. I imagined it was one of those places that stayed open late and served pancakes to truckers. We had met once, the first day I moved in. She stopped to help me with a box of pots and pans I had dropped. Her name tag said 'Margaret' but she wrinkled her nose and insisted anyone under 50 should just call her Maggie.

I had barely said a word to her, too stressed out and unsure what to say. Here we were, already starting the fall semester, and I was still waiting for a good time to introduce myself again. She seemed about my age, another girl living alone, we already had things in common, maybe she would want to get coffee sometime.

But, hiding behind a door in pajamas with a fried-rice carton full of frogs was probably not the time to ask.

I watched Maggie walk through the courtyard, stopping to peek into the fountain. She stayed there for a minute before she opened the door across the square from mine and went inside. Maggie's apartment was directly across from mine and I knew from experience that pretty soon her light would be on and I'd be able to see right into her apartment.

I turned my attention back to the wet, croaking box in my hands. I quickly went back to my own apartment, flicking on my own lights. I rushed past the window and to the bathroom. I dumped the container of frogs into my tub and ran the faucet until they had a good amount of water. There were a couple clumps of moss stuck to my shirt from the fountain. I plucked them off and dropped them into the bath with the frogs. All of them were still and quiet, taking in their surroundings. They were a bit small, but all were bright green and seemed healthy enough for living in a gross fountain.

"Be good," I waved a finger threateningly at them. "I'll be back to check on you."

In the kitchen, I opened up the fridge to look over my poor offerings. I doubted frogs were supposed to eat peanut butter, pickles, or eggs. Actually, I had no idea what they ate besides bugs. I still hadn't called to get my internet fixed, so there was no way of searching for it.

It would be fine, as soon as the sun was up I'd go take them to the park down the street. They could live in a big pond and have all the bugs and whatever else they wanted. For now, I washed the sticky feeling of cardboard off my hands. I was too wound up to sleep, so I put a mug of water in the microwave and resolved to finally finish unpacking.

While my water was heating up, I heard a thud from outside and I walked over to my window to look out. Across the courtyard, Maggie had opened up her window and was shaking out a blanket. I stepped back so she wouldn't see me watching her finish and turned back out of view, leaving the window open.

Everything in her apartment was colorful. I could see the edge of her kitchen counter, wrapped in a strand of fairy lights, purple and yellow bowls sitting on top, filled with apples and grapes. On the wall was a tapestry of woven threads and yarn, not making any specific picture, just an explosion of color, spreading across the wall and dripping down to rest on top of her couch, which was a bright, velvety teal. She had lime green curtains which were pushed aside most days so I could see her walk back and forth with a steaming mug or bag of chips in her hand.

My own apartment was blank. Perfectly white walls and a dark, wood floor covered in scratches and dust, buried between layers of lacquer. My worn, red comforter thrown over my mattress was the only pop of color besides my scattered mugs and dirty clothes. I had left most of my stuff at home. When I thought I would be staying in a dorm, I figured it wasn't worth the hassle, packing everything up, moving it in, doing it all again in a year. Except now, being in my own space, it felt so empty all the time, sort of like I was melting into the blankness, like one day I'd wake up and find myself just another piece of dust glued onto the floor.

I wondered what Maggie thought when she looked in here, or if she ever did. Back home, my room was covered in posters and half-finished paintings made at sleepovers. My window was taped up from where it had cracked during a bad winter. When I looked out, I could see the woods and the tall grasses that covered them, coming up to my waist when I went out for walks. The only grass around here was all flooded and muddy from the rain we'd been having.

The microwave dinged, I dissolved a spoonful of instant coffee into my mug, then got to work building my desk. I was roughly halfway through when soft croaking erupted from the bathroom. I ripped off a chunk of cardboard box and went to check on the frogs. They were still sitting in the tub, staring up at me. I placed the cardboard in the tub so it floated, a makeshift lilypad.

"Here, you guys have pool toys now," one frog hopped on it immediately. It looked up at me, puffing out its chest and croaking loudly.

"Yeah, you're welcome, but don't get too comfortable." The frog hopped back into the water, leaving a small clump of moss behind. There was actually a considerable amount of moss in my tub now, it almost looked like it was covering the bottom. How did a few frogs track in that much crap? I'd have to remember to pick up some shower cleaner after going to the park. And some groceries.

With the frogs hopefully entertained, I continued to wrestle with my desk. I could still hear croaking from the bathroom, but the door muffled most of it. Faint music came from outside, probably Maggie since we seemed to be the only people up so late. I sat up on my knees and took another peek out my window. Maggie had her hair wrapped up in a towel and a nightshirt on with her bare legs sticking out. She was swaying side to side, mouthing the words to the song playing. I didn't recognize it.

Maggie turned towards the window and I dropped down onto my mattress to avoid being caught. I should just stand up and wave. Say, *Hi, do you know much about frogs? It seems like we both stay up late. Would you like to get some coffee?*

It would be nice to have a friend here. Most of my classes were in huge rooms filled with people who all seemed to have their groups made up. The girl who had the desk-shift on campus before me was nice, but she never stuck around long to talk. After I unpacked and got my place looking a little less awful, maybe I could invite Maggie over. I could buy a poster and stick it up on the wall where she could see it through the window. Then, at least I'd have an icebreaker.

I turned back to my desk but saw that another clump of moss was stuck to the side of one panel. I must have had some stuck to my hands. It wouldn't peel off either, I'd need to scrub it with something. I really thought I had gotten all the moss off of me, but looking down I saw there was a spread of it on my shirt, gross and damp.

I got some paper towels wet under the sink and started rubbing the moss away. It seemed like no matter how hard I scrubbed, it wouldn't come off. What the hell was this stuff? Some sort of mutant, frog residue? I stopped trying to get it off and just took the shirt off to go find another from my floor. My desk, which moments before only had one small clump on the side, was now completely covered. Squishy, green fuzz coated it like I had pulled it out of a bog. The moss was spreading.

I ran back to my bathroom and threw open the door. My bathtub was overgrown with the stuff. I couldn't see any porcelain. There were whole vines too, dangling from my shower rod, wrapping around and poking through the curtain. I had no idea where they had rooted.

Three of the frogs were still sitting in the tub, unbothered by the shift in surroundings. The other two were sitting in the sink, which was now also filled with water despite both taps being turned off. It had a yellow, marshy top to it that was sloshing onto the floor. The frogs were all still croaking. I backed up and shut the door.

Okay. Okay, okay, okay. I shut my eyes and squeezed them tightly. There was not a marsh in my bathroom. I had only been gone for about half an hour. I was obviously hallucinating from lack of sleep and stress. Or there was a gas leak. Or my Thai food had been drugged with hallucinogens. All I had to do was take a deep breath, clear my mind, and open the door. I pressed my forehead to the frame, taking one last deep breath. I grabbed the doorknob firmly and pulled.

Cold water rushed past me and into the hallway, sloshing over my feet. With it came a few small, silver-scaled fish and clumps of uprooted ferns and grass.

Inside the bathroom, cattails and ferns had sprung up, surrounding what used to be my tub. Water was overflowing from the sink and winding its way between plants, like a river, out into my hallway. The bathroom floor was covered in mud, moss, and the roots of trees. Whole trees, in my bathroom, that pushed up against the ceiling and formed a canopy of dense green leaves. More vines wrapped around my vanity lights and the door, dangling down in my face.

The frogs were croaking loudly from somewhere inside, but I couldn't see them anymore. The sound was joined by buzzing dragonflies that had begun circling the room. I backed up and slipped on the wet floor, landing on my butt in the shallow swamp. My whole apartment was going to flood if I couldn't figure out how to stop this. There were no taps running that I could see, but the water was still coming. I shut the door again firmly and squashed back into my living room in my wet shorts and tank top.

My phone was sitting on top of the kitchen counter, dry and unharmed. The moss from my desk had spread across the floor. Already, my mattress had been swallowed by a mass of weeds and roots. There was a thin layer of boggy water steadily rising around me with tall grasses springing up along my walls.

A frog hopped up onto the counter, startling me into dropping my phone into the now shin-deep water. I watched as what looked like a catfish swam by and swallowed it whole. The frog croaked once before hopping down. There were a couple more frogs swimming. One was resting on a piece of driftwood that was floating near my mattress. I looked back towards the bathroom and heard the same muffled croaking as before.

I stumbled my way towards the front door. Cattails brushed against my legs and I pushed them away. A small, brown bird landed on top of one of them, eyeing some of the beetles that were floating in the water below. It chirped shrilly at me and I backed away.

I pulled open the door and stepped into the hallway, slamming it shut again behind me before too much water could escape. Thank God I didn't have downstairs neighbors. It didn't look like anything was leaking out. I felt around at the bottom of the door and pressed my ear against it, listening for any wildlife or rushing water, but couldn't hear anything through the wood.

My legs were soaked, and my shorts were dripping onto the hall carpet. I tried to wipe off any clumps of moss and grass that had stuck to me. They fell to the floor and stayed, not growing any further. I looked back at my apartment, hand hovering over the door once more, before dropping it. I walked down the hall and around the corner on shaky legs and damp, bare feet. I knew when I had found the right door. It had polka dot wrapping paper taped all over it with a plastic, glittery welcome mat. I wrapped my knuckles softly against the door.

Maggie pulled the door open. She was in her nightshirt with dots of acne cream dabbed on her face. She stared at me.

"You live across the square from me, right?" she asked eventually.

"Yeah," I replied. "I'm Sylvia."

"Right, what's up? Is it raining again or something? You're like, super wet."

"Can I come in?" I asked. Maggie's eyebrows shot up. "I know it's really late. I've had sort of a weird night."

"Okay, yeah." We continued to stand in the hall staring at each other. Maggie shifted on the balls of her feet, "Come on in." She moved to the side, and I walked past her, careful not to brush her with my damp arm.

The wood floor was similar to mine, but Maggie's was covered in mismatched rugs, and the plain walls were hidden by bookcases littered with trinkets, from a tambourine to a collection of small, porcelain houses. I stood stiffly in the entrance, hoping I wasn't dripping too badly onto her pretty rugs. "Here, one second," Maggie seemed to notice my discomfort. She disappeared around the corner and came back with a yellow, fluffy towel that she handed to me.

"Thank you."

"Sure. Here, dry off, I'll make some popcorn?"

"That'd be great, thanks." I rubbed the towel over my legs, arms, and then hair.

"Hey, do you like coffee?" I raised my head up from toweling off my hair. Maggie was smiling at me, waiting for a reply. I realized she had wiped off her acne cream.

"Yeah, coffee is good. Thanks, again." Maggie nodded and moved away to rummage around in her cabinets. I held my used towel tightly in my arms.

Across the room, Maggie's window looked out onto the courtyard, same as mine did. I peered out at the dark square of grass and the empty, silent fountain in the center. The lights in my apartment were still on, creating a glowing spot of empty, white wall. I couldn't see anything else. No birds, no vines, no rising water. Maggie's coffee maker beeped, startling me away from my absorption in the scene. Maggie called me over to pick out a mug and I went, begrudgingly turning away from the window. I left it open, letting in the sounds of cars rushing past outside and the distant sound of croaking.

Previous Publication Notes

Thank you to the journals who have previously housed
my work online.

Camas Magazine
The Bookends Review
Chaotic Merge Magazine
Red Ogre Review
Cosmic Double Magazine